THE GREAT GORGONZOLA HEIST

by D T Lofthouse

CHAPTERS

Big Ideas   5
The Climb   12
Snuggles   21
Then There Were Four   26
Sort of A Plan   31
Hole Sweet Hole   34
Come on Donnie   40
New for Old Plan   43
Surprise   51
Supplies   57
Lettuce Pray   62
Waiting for Dotty   66
The Plan Unfolded   68
Friend or Foe   78
Gregory's Wall   85
In the Factory   93
The Cheese Store   101
Pipes Away   117
Quick, to the Rat Cave   125
Time to Head Home   131

Chapter 1

BIG IDEAS?

Once upon a Monday, you know, the day after Sunday but before Tuesday, anyway, it was a day none the less.

It was a cold, Autumnal day, but not quite freezing. "Squeak!", came a voice from the rabbit hole next to the toilet, followed by "damn and blast, we need to get a new ladder down there!!".   I was listening to the drama unfolding from a little distance away.

Mmmm? Why is there a Rabbit hole next to the toilet?? I thought to myself.   I had thought this on many occasions but still had no idea.

It was the voice of Bert, a field mouse, he'd been adopted by the Albino's, the Rabbit family that lived in the Rabbit hole, they were like the Mafia.
Bert was hiding in the shadows because the Albino's didn't know he was out after lights out, which was around 6 in the evening.

Now, that is quite unusual, as Rabbits and Mice usually come out at night to 'hunt'.
How they hunt for cheese or carrots is beyond me.

Bert, couldn't sleep, he was laying in his oversized matchbox bed, staring at the soil ceiling of the Rabbit hole, thinking about the huge piece of Gorgonzola he had dreamt about, he decided to get up and go out of the rabbit hole.

"How can I get my paws on that pongy cheese?" he thought to himself.   I knew what Bert was thinking because he often thought aloud, you could hear a kind of whirring sound, like a clock spinning without counting time, which usually meant he was planning something.

His hair-brained schemes didn't always go to plan and that's the reason little Joey Albino was spending his life behind the bars of a Rabbit hutch, under the watchful eye of Gregory, the snotty kid that lives next to the carrot farm.
Another one of Bert's foiled plans.

Bert was the biggest mouse in his family, well, he was the only mouse in his original family after the horrific combined harvester incident of 1998 in the wheat field next to the carrot farm. Bert was always planning things that occasionally paid-off, like the almost famous loaf robbery of 2005, in which he got away with granary and wholemeal loaf quite unscathed.

Suddenly, a larger than mouse nose popped out of the Rabbit hole, twitching and sniffing the evening air, with the occasional snuffled noise for good measure.

It was the nose belonging to Donnie Albino, little Joeys younger brother. He had also heard Bert thinking aloud and usually tried to stop his plans before they got off to a not so flying start, especially after what had happened to little Joey. As everyone knows, Rabbits, not just the Albino's, were BIG families.

Donnie couldn't have his family getting any smaller, even though he had hundreds of brothers and sisters living elsewhere.
"What are you up to Bert?" asked Donnie.

"Erm, well, nothing?!" answered Bert hurriedly. "Come on, I know you Bert, you're always up to one thing or another", Donnie said.

"Okay, okay. I'm planning a cheese heist, the greatest cheese heist known to all mouse-kind" replied Bert confidently, well, as confidently as any mouse could, when talking to an Albino, even though he was family now.

"But we need to get little Joey sprung from the hutch", he added.

"You know little Joey is in the hutch for life", said Donnie.

Bert knew that little Joey was the best at what he did, they had planned the loaf robbery together and little Joey allowed Bert take all the credit for the plan. They had done many heists without the other Albino's knowledge, even though they thought they knew everything that happened in the family.

Little Joey was always getting into trouble when he and Bert were together, Bert was a bad influence, well, they were a bad influence on each other.

'So, to the plan', thought Bert, he was thinking aloud again.

"Donnie!" said Bert, "here's what we need to do".

"Oh no", Donnie snapped.

"Now shhh! And listen", responded Bert with an air of authority or an air of wind, not sure which but one doesn't smell like rotten cabbages in the compost heap.

I couldn't smell cabbages, so it must have been an air of authority.

Donnie just stopped, pricked up his huge, usually floppy ears, "Go on then smarty pants, what's the plan?" said Donnie.

Bert was surprised at Donnie's reaction, as he would usually get a swift kick in the bum for raising his voice to any of the Albino's.

Except little Joey, they were best friends as well as brothers.

"We will wait until the village church bells chime 12, we'll sneak out of the Rabbit hole, across the carrot farm and into Gregory's garden", said Bert.

"But won't it be light outside Bert?" replied Donnie.

"No!! I mean 12 midnight, not lunchtime",
hissed Bert, getting frustrated with him, Donnie
didn't have a clue about telling the time or even
counting the chimes of the church bell due to his
short attention span.

His dad, big Joey said that he was part Rabbit
and part Goldfish, with a memory to match!

The day passed relatively swiftly, Donnie and
Bert were preparing for the breakout of Little
Joey just outside the rabbit hole and out of
earshot of the rest of the Albinos. "Have you got
the string Donnie?" asked Bert.
"What do we need string for? Are we tying up
the kid who has Little Joey?" Donnie replied all
excited.
"No! We need it to climb the wall of the Carrot
farm" responded Bert "we don't need a hostage
Donnie, we're trying to free Little Joey".
"Oh, I forget" said Donnie, somewhat
disappointed.

They had some string, the hook part of an old
coat hanger, to use with the string, to climb the
wall of the carrot farm, the toes of a pair of old
socks as a sort of balaclava disguise, a couple of
matches to use as flares in case of emergency

and a safety pin to pick the padlock of the rabbit hutch.

"Synchronise watches" said Donnie.
"I can't carry a watch, I'm a field mouse if you have forgotten", scowled Bert, "besides, why have you got a watch when you don't know how to tell the time?" he added whilst chuckling to himself.
"It was a present!" Donnie snapped, getting a bit annoyed at Bert.

Chapter 2

THE CLIMB

The time had come, the church bells had begun their midnight chimes, "Right" said Bert, "better get a move on or we'll never get this Hutch break done". The pair set off into the moonlit night, scurrying under the brambles to hide themselves from the huge barn owl that patrolled the fields every night.

They had gotten quite far on the route to the carrot farm, when they heard and almighty "Twit Twoo" from above their heads, they stopped suddenly. "W-W-What was that" asked Donnie, shaking in his fur, he didn't get out much.
"Shhh! It's the owl in the branches, it will hear you", whispered Bert in his amazement that

Donnie hadn't heard nor seen the owl before now. They stood, frozen to the spot in fear.
"What now?" Donnie asked.
"Now we wait", replied Bert "and keep your voice down".

Just as Bert had finished talking, they saw the owl fly off into the darkness of the woods behind the carrot farm.

"Come on Donnie, it is safe for now but keep a look out in case it comes back".

They ventured a little further towards the carrot farm and Gregory's garden where Little Joey was captive in the hutch, over huge mountainous rocks.

The rocks were merely stones that had fallen from the wall at the other side of the bramble and somehow tumbled underneath.

"Come on, you're starting to lag behind, we don't have much time, especially if the owl comes back" said Bert. With that, Donnie let out a frightened squeak and hopped faster towards

Bert, who had already scurried in front by a couple of metres. "I don't know if I can take much more" gasped Donnie, who was by now, petrified of anything that moved in the dark night sky.

"What do you mean?" said Bert, "just hop a little faster".

"That's easy for you to say, I'm hopping as fast as I can after I ate that carrot casserole that mama made", replied Donnie.
Mama, otherwise known as Mrs Albino, did have a first name but only big Joey was allowed to say it.

She was a rabbit that you could not argue with, if she told you to "eat your carrot casserole", you would reply "how much mama?" or risk getting hit with the uncooked carrots that were left over for the next casserole!

Now, there's a lot I know about the Albino's, but I can't tell you who I am yet, let's just say I can get around without being seen or heard.
"You shouldn't eat a big meal before a job

Donnie, it slows you down" said Bert all knowing, as Little Joey had already told him the same on their many adventures

"I was hungry Bert, you know I can't resist carrot casserole like you can't resist corn cobbler" replied Donnie thinking back to the hours previous, slightly drooling at the thought of more carrot casserole.

"Donnie! We haven't got time for this, we're nearly at the carrot farm wall" shouted Bert when he realised Donnie had gone into food flashback.

On they went, over more mountainous rocks and under various shrubbery along the way, keeping a look out for the owl at every step, scurry and hop.
"Bert, stop!" shouted Donnie.
"What's wrong now?" said Bert getting, irritated at the thought of yet another setback.
"Where's the bag we set off with?" questioned Donnie, somewhat confused.
"It's still on your back!" Bert replied, getting more irritated.
"Oh, yeah", Donnie replied with relief, "come on then Bert, what are we waiting for?!" not realising that it was he who had stopped them.

It was a short time until they reached the wall of the carrot farm, after a few scares from the owl whilst crossing the wheat field.

Donnie was still shaking in his fur from the first time the owl was menstioned.
"Ok Donnie, this is what we need to do now", said Bert, his heart pounding with excitement.

"Get the hook and string from the bag", he added.

Donnie didn't quite understand what they were doing with the string and old piece of coat hanger.

Bert tied the string to the hook using a technique that he had learned in the Mouse Brigade.   A mouse equivalent to the boy scouts or girl guides, if you were a girl mouse.
"What now?" Donnie said, looking a little bewildered.
"I need you to throw the hook as high as you can, so we can climb the wall", replied Bert, handing him the hook and string.

With this, Donnie threw the hook high into the air with all the effort of two rabbits. The hook fell back to the ground with a CLUNK!
"No, no, no", said Bert, as Donnie had thrown the hook straight upwards with no aim towards the wall they needed to climb. "Try again, this time, towards the top of the wall".
The second attempt was on target.

The hook landing with a reassuring thud, just over the top of the carrot farm wall. "Now,

Donnie, give it a sharp tug", Bert told him.
Donnie, pulled in the string as Bert had told him,
"and now what Bert? It's stuck!" he said.
"That's the idea, now climb it!" Bert said.

Donnie took hold of the string in both paws and
with an almighty heave, he managed to climb all
of two inches.
"This is hard work Bert", he gasped.
He continued to pull himself up the string with
all the effort he could find, eventually getting to
the top.
"Your turn Bert", he panted, out of breath from
the ordeal.   Bert took hold of the string and
began to climb, using a method that he, again,
had learned in the Mouse Brigade. He was a
little quicker up the string than Donnie because
mice were naturally good climbers.

At the top, Bert said to Donnie, who was still
gasping for air and laid on his back tired from all
the activity, "we have to turn the hook around
and climb down the other side now, into the
carrot farm", "but we have to watch out for
Snuggles".
"Snuggles?   Who or what is Snuggles?", asked
Donnie, very confused due to being breathless
and extremely out of touch with reality.

"Snuggles, my dear brother, is the guard dog that patrols the carrot farm at night", replied Bert.

Just as Bert was explaining to Donnie about Snuggles, they heard a "WOOSH" noise above their heads, it was the owl, luckily for them, it had not seen them on top of the wall.
"Donnie", whispered Bert very panicked.
"What is wrong with you Bert? Still out of breath?" replied Donnie smugly, as he was no longer out of breath.
"D-D-Didn't you hear the owl?" asked Bert
"Erm, no?! Where is it?" Donnie asked, looking around in the darkness.
"It just flew passed our heads again, that was close, we really have to get a move on now, I would rather face Snuggles than that owl", Bert said.

Bert moved the hook to the opposite side of the wall and told Donnie that he has to climb down, being careful not to burn his paws on the string on the way down.
He thought he understood what Bert meant, although he probably didn't.

He slowly lowered himself down the string, paw under paw he went, hearing what Bert had said playing over in his mind.   The fact was, Bert was whispering repeatedly what he had said, over and over, so Donnie didn't forget.

A few minutes had passed, Donnie had now reached the ground. "Right Bert, your turn", said Donnie in a sort of shouting whisper so he didn't attract the attention of the owl or Snuggles. Bert lowered himself onto the string to climb down, "Wait!" Donnie squeaked, "I hear something".

Bert stopped, suspended over the edge of the wall, waiting to start the climb down, "okay, the coast is clear" said Donnie.
Bert carried on down the string towards the ground, it was only a matter of seconds but felt much longer to Donnie, waiting, ears pricked up. Which was quite an effort, EVERYTHING was an effort to Donnie.
"What is the next step?" asked Donnie.
"We need to try and get the hook down so we can use it on Gregory's wall then we only have the hutch to tackle", Bert replied, "come on before Snuggles sees us or the owl comes back".

Bert gave a quick flick of the string and the hook came tumbling from the top of the wall, hitting Donnie square on the ears, "Ouch!!" he protested, "That hurt".   As Bert gathered up the string and hook to put back into the rucksack.

They set off towards the wall of Gregory's garden. Half way to the wall, Snuggles came bounding out of the shadows of the kennel that was his home. Within seconds, he was in front of the, now petrified, pair.

Chapter 3

SNUGGLES

"Grrrr", said Snuggles, "where are you going and why are you on my patch?" he growled. "I should just gobble you up!" snarling at them. Donnie and Bert just looked at each other, not knowing what to do, then, all of a sudden, they heard a loud swooshing noise, watching as the ground slowly disappeared from beneath their feet, thankfully in the direction of Gregory's garden.

The owl had swooped down and picked up Bert and Donnie, literally right from under Snuggles' nose. "Donnie", said Bert, "I think this is the end, it's been nice to be part of a family again". "Really?" replied Donnie "the end? As in THE end? But we haven't rescued little Joey from the hutch yet".

Bert was about to say something else as he felt them nearing the ground, then PLONK! They dropped from a small height. "OUCH!!" said Donnie and Bert together.

The owl landed in front of them, staring at the shocked pair with his menacing eyes.

"W-W-Who are you?" asked the owl. Bert and Donnie looked at each other for a few moments, then Bert piped up, "I'm Bert Albino and this is Donnie Albino, you don't want to hurt us or you will be in trouble with our Family".

He was trying to be brave, in the hope that the owl would think twice about eating them.

"Hoo Hoo Hoo", laughed the owl.

Owls do have a sense of humour and always laughed like that, it's what owls do.

"Bert my dear boy, I have no intention of eating you, I saved you from Snuggles and for me, that was scary enough without having to tackle a mouse and rabbit for my supper" said the Owl.

"My name is Godfrey Brown, but my friends call me Dotty, on account of my feather pattern" said Dotty.

"I had overheard of your mission to rescue little Joey from the hutch when I was flying over the corn field two nights ago and was going to help but every time I got close enough to ask, you both panicked and ran away. Picking you up from in front of Snuggles was a little unexpected" said Dotty.

"Big Joey and I go way back, I remember him when he was a teenage bunny and helped in the rescue of Bert when his family...well, you know the rest Bert" Dotty continued.

"So, that means...you saved me and Big Joey adopted me?" said Bert in shock.

"Thank you, Mr Brown, thank you indeed", he added gratefully.

"It was my pleasure young Bert and please, call me Dotty", Dotty said.

"Let's get the safety pin out and have a go at the padlock of the hutch" said Bert.

Donnie, Dotty and Bert, with safety pin in paw, hopped, scampered and skipped towards the hutch.   He was an expert at unlocking padlocks with a pin, after several times of being locked up himself, but that's another story.   As they approached the hutch, out popped a wet, whisker surrounded nose.

"Who's there?" asked a voice from the hutch, it was quite a relief for them to hear little Joey after such a long time.   He'd been held captive for about two weeks, which was a very long time in rabbit or mouse terms, but not that long for owls, that's how they become so wise.

"It's Bert", answered Bert.

"Bert who?" he replied, vaguely.

"Little Joey, it's me, Bert, Bert Albino, your brother?" he said, saddened that little Joey had forgotten him already.

"Ah! I was just making sure Bert, you've got to be careful these days, you never know who you could be talking to, I hope you understand", said little Joey reassuringly.

"Phew! I thought you had forgotten me", Bert replied, "I'm with Donnie and Dotty".

"So you've met Dotty, I've only heard about him, when I was a little bunny, Papa used to tell us stories at bedtime" little Joey said.

"I am he, nice to meet you in the fur" Dotty said, skipping closer to the hutch.

"it's my pleasure to meet you Dotty, I have heard so much about you and those stories have seen me through lots of scrapes and fur raising times", replied little Joey.

"Are we going to release little Joey or what?!" said Donnie impatiently, "we can talk more when we are safely at the rabbit hole".

Bert was quite surprised at the reaction of Donnie but agreed with him and the sense that he had made. It was unusual for Donnie to make any sense at all.

Bert unfolded the safety pin, which was quite some effort, approached the lock of the rabbit hutch and proceeded to wiggle the pin in the keyhole. He wiggled it this way, wiggled it that way, back and forth for what seemed like ages.

Finally, he heard a loud click and the lock sprung open, nearly throwing him from the piece of wood that he was balanced on.
Bert lifted the lock from the clasp of the rabbit hutch door, then jumped down from the wooden ledge. Little Joey nudged open the door, hopping out, in front of Bert, Donnie and Dotty. He stood on his hind legs, stretching due to being squashed in the rabbit hutch.

Chapter 4
THEN THERE WERE FOUR

"Bert, what are we to do now?" asked Dotty, "you're the mastermind behind this escape".
"It took us quite some time to get to the carrot farm and over the wall, but when you picked us up and brought us into Gregory's garden, that time went quickly", Bert said, "so, my original plan of getting back the same way has change"
"So, come on Bert, what's the new plan?", asked Dotty
"Well, obviously, it all depends on you", said Bert.

Dotty looked a little confused at this, but decided to hear the idea that Bert had come up with.
"Go on Bert, what?"   Dotty said, now somewhat more interested.   He hadn't been part of any plan for a very long time.
"This is my idea, if you can carry Little Joey and

Donnie in your claws, carefully, I will hold onto your leg and you fly us all back to the rabbit hole?", Bert suggested, grinning at his own genius.   He thought the plan was fool proof and therefore brilliant.

"Mmmm, so let me get this straight, I pick them up in my claws and you hold onto one of my legs?", said Dotty, making sure he had heard Bert correctly.

"Exactly!", said Bert, still grinning at the thought that it could work.

Gregory's bedroom light flickered into life, the group hopped, fluttered and scurried into a dark corner of the garden so they wouldn't be seen if Gregory looked from the window. The light went out, as quickly as it came on.

"That was close", said little Joey, looking at the rest of the escape party, all standing in the dark, hearts pounding.

"Quickly!", said Dotty, "we have to put Bert's plan into action before we are seen or worse, caught"

He flapped his huge wings, hovering just enough to be able to pick up Donnie and little Joey, "Bert, you will have to climb up, over Donnie, once he is in place", Dotty said.

Donnie and little Joey positioned themselves under Dotty, waiting for what they thought could be a painful journey. Dotty, grabbed hold of them, gently with his talons, then nodded to Bert to climb aboard.   His nodding was more of a twist of the head than a nod, owls weren't good at nodding.

Bert climbed up Donnie's nose, onto his neck and positioned himself around Dotty's leg.
"That tickles Bert", giggled Donnie.
Bert didn't quite understand why Donnie was giggling.
"Oops, sorry Donnie, I've just realised", Bert said, quickly removing his foot from Donnie's ear.
"It's ok Bert, it was quite funny actually", chuckled Donnie.

"Shhh!", said little Joey, "Dotty has to concentrate and doesn't want you two putting him off".
"Sorry Dotty", said the pair together, neither of them could really see Dotty's face, just the mass of feathers that were on his chest.
"It's ok boys, I've flown under worse conditions than this", Dotty hooted, "hold on tight Bert", he

added.

With a few flaps of his wings, they were up in the air, high above the garden and could just make out Snuggles in the darkness, he still looked as though he didn't know what had happened earlier.

It took a matter of minutes to fly the distance it had taken Bert and Donnie half the night to travel.

Dotty slowly lowered Bert, Donnie and little Joey near the rabbit hole but not too close that they could wake big Joey, he would be quite cross that he was not included in their recent escapade.

"Don't forget to include me in your next adventure", hooted Dotty with excitement in his hoot, giving Bert a little wink.

Little Joey looked at Bert with a look that could only be described as bewildered and empty.

"Well, ahem", spluttered Bert, his face starting show signs of him hiding something.

Little Joey was unaware of any plans, let alone the one that Bert had been thinking of.

"What's he talking about Bert?" said little Joey, even more bewildered than he was a couple of minutes ago.

Bert stood there, at a loss for words as little Joey
stared at him, while Dotty had a look of 'oh no
what have I said!' on his feathery beak.
"Well Bert?" questioned little Joey.

Chapter 5

SORT OF A PLAN

"It's like this little Joey" Bert began, "I was thinking of a cheese heist at the Gorgonzola factory but the plan needs a bit of polishing around the edges", he added, not knowing how little Joey would react after the last plan had landed him in Gregory's rabbit hutch.
"Mmm, so you think we should break into the Gorgonzola factory then Bert?", asked little Joey, "but the rest of the Albinos don't eat cheese, just you!", he added.

Bert looked at little Joey quite surprised, "erm, yes?" he replied in a questioning manner.
"Ok, we'll plan the heist properly", said little Joey with a slight grin.
"But the way you said that I was the only one who ate cheese, I thought you didn't want to do the heist"
"No, no Bert, I was just playing", said little Joey, "how much of the plan have you got so far?"

"The plan starts similar to how we came to break you out, I have planned as far as the carrot farm but when I started planning, we didn't have the help of Dotty or you for certain.   So, now, we have to start a new plan to include you and Dotty" said Bert

"Hang on a carrot munching minute!", exclaimed Donnie, " where do I fit into this grand idea?".

"Donnie, you do fit into the plan but we need to start it again, but, with the help of little Joey, there will be less risk and with Dotty, we get things done quicker", said Bert.

"Oh, ok", said Donnie, not wanting to miss out.

He saw it as an adventure, rather than a job, even though they were really stealing Gorgonzola from the factory.   With that little outburst and explanation, Donnie sat back down near the rabbit hole and listened carefully, waiting for Bert to come out with the greatest idea ever. Any idea is great to Donnie, he wasn't really an ideas rabbit.

"Right, boys", said Bert, "time for bed, we'll plan the rest when we have slept"

"Plan the rest?" little Joey said, "we haven't planned anything if this is going to be a new plan Bert", he added, waiting for the quick answer that he thought Bert would throw at him. But nothing, not a sound, Bert was fast asleep already.

Dotty had been waiting for a chance to leave and this was it, "Donnie, little Joey, I'm off", Dotty said, he skipped in a sort of half circle, readying himself for take-off, "the same time tomorrow?", he asked.
"You can come around as the church bells strike midnight and thanks again", little Joey said.
"Ok, Cheerio and toodles", Dotty said, a few flaps of his wings and he was off again, into the darkness of the early hours.
"Donnie, pick Bert up gently, take him into the rabbit hole and put him to bed", little Joey told him.

Donnie knew he wasn't allowed to argue with little Joey because he was older, it was the Albino way. Older members of the family had to lead the younger ones, passing on their experience and knowledge.
Donnie picked up Bert in his mouth by the scruff of the neck, like dogs do with their puppies.
"Night little Joey, we've missed you", Donnie mumbled.   It must be hard to speak with a mouthful of mouse.

Chapter 6
HOLE SWEET HOLE

Little Joey, sat outside the rabbit hole, looking at the morning sky, with dawn fast approaching and thinking that it had been quite an eventful day. One minute locked up in a hutch and the next, flying under Dotty.

He let out a big sigh, he was clearly happy and thankful that he was home. Although, he wasn't sure what morning would bring because big Joey didn't know he was going to be broken out of the hutch. So many thoughts racing around, little Joey leant back against the toilet next to the rabbit hole, closed his eyes and fell fast asleep.

As the morning arrived, Bert and Donnie woke almost at the same time, the autumn, sun shining a glimmer of light down the rabbit hole, close to where they were sleeping.
"Oh", yawned Donnie, "I'm still tired Bert".
"Me too", replied Bert, "we've only had a few hours and really need to save our energy for this evening, I'm so hungry".

With that, the pair got out of their beds and headed for the store cupboard. This was a hole in the middle of the rabbit hole's maze of tunnels and it didn't even have a door, so it was more of a store hole than a cupboard.

Donnie took out a couple of carrot biscuits on which he placed lettuce leaf dressing because the biscuits would otherwise be too dry.
Bert reached in and pulled out a large piece of corn-jack, a bit like flapjack, but made with corn kernels, another of Mrs Albinos specialities.
They hopped and scurried back to bed to munch on their favourite snacks. If big Joey knew they were eating in bed he would be telling them off and reminding them that food should be eaten in the kitchen, dining room or outside, not in bed.
No sooner had they finished their snacks, they both fell asleep again.

While they sleep, I'll tell you a little about me. My name is Tony Gambino, most of the animals used to know me as Tony "The Rat" on account that I'm a rat. When I say 'used to', I mean, before I was missing in action. I now live in the head of the scarecrow, it's a good place to keep a lookout without being seen and it's safe for me, I don't want to blow my cover.

I've been watching little Joey, Donnie and Bert for most of their lives, with the help of my military training in the SRS, Special Rat Service, where I had specialised in intelligence and communications, so I could lip read and set up equipment to spy on the enemy.

Last night was quite a difficult task for me, but thanks to the listening devices I had placed around the fields, it wasn't impossible.

Listening devices were mainly made up of plastic cups and strings, which had taken years to place around the rabbit hole and fields, sometimes having to make the same sort of journeys that Bert and Donnie had made. I stood watch over Bert and Donnie during the escape plan of little Joey with the help of some binoculars I made from a couple of thimbles that people had thrown away.

Now to the reason that I have been watching them. Big Joey and I go a long way back, we've been friends since being young, playing in the fields of Naples, then we got separated when I joined the SRS. It took a while to find him again.

We grew up in the Verminage, like an orphanage that humans have, both our parents had died in accidents, big Joey's parents died running from hedge to hedge on the country roads, the driver didn't see them and my parents were poisoned, they were only trying to eat.

He looked after me in the Verminage and I vowed that I would, one day, return the favour. Big Joey also met his wife, Fiorela in the Verminage too.

I think Bert, Donnie, little Joey and Dotty may need my help with the heist they're but I'm not coming out of hiding just yet.

As the day went on and the night grew ever closer, Bert and Donnie started to wake up, sort of thinking about the plan ahead, but certainly talking of food again.

"I'm hungry", said Donnie, looking at Bert as if he wanted to eat him.

"Me too", replied Bert, looking at Donnie the same way.

"Come on Bert, I think Mama made a carrot casserole last night, I could smell it when we came back", Donnie said, drooling yet again.

Sleep and food were pretty much all Donnie was interested in.

Bert could eat carrot casserole but corn cobbler was just irresistible, "I hope there's a bit of corn cobbler left over from last week", said Bert.
"Bert, surely that would have gone mouldy by now", Donnie said, his stomach turning at the thought.
"Doesn't matter Donnie, it adds to the flavour", Bert replied, winking at him.   It was more of a twitch, Bert had never been able to wink properly.

They hopped and scurried through the maze of the rabbit hole, back to the store cupboard. Luckily, they both found what they had hoped for, although Bert would have preferred a bigger piece, he had to make do with the corn cobbler that was left.
Surprisingly, it wasn't too moldy but much more tasty with the mold than it normally was.

Big Joey and Mama Albino were hopping about the rabbit hole when Bert saw them, "Have you seen little Joey?" asked Bert.
Big Joey and Mama just looked at each other with a kind of 'has he lost his marbles?!' expression on their faces.
"Don't you remember Bert?" replied Big Joey, "he's in the rabbit hutch for life".

"Oh, yes!" said Bert, "I-I-I almost forgot".
Big Joey was suspicious at the way Bert
answered due to the fact that he was only at a
loss for words on two occasions.   One, he
would be scared and the other, he was trying to
hide something.   He WAS hiding something.

Chapter 7
COME ON DONNIE

Bert went back through the maze of the rabbit hole to find Donnie, eventually finding him, laid down on his bed.   Which was the lid of an old shoe box, lined with material that was once part of a picnic blanket.
"Come on Donnie, it's getting dark and we need to get things moving", Bert said eagerly.
"But I'm still tired", replied Donnie, trying to hide under the bed covers eating carrot casserole.

Eventually, Donnie got himself out of bed whilst Bert was scurrying around, gathering supplies for the heist.
"We need to find little Joey", whispered Bert to Donnie, the pair went up and out of the rabbit hole.   Little Joey was still fast asleep, he had woken briefly through the day to eat, then fell asleep again as Bert and Donnie had done in the rabbit hole.

"Are you awake?" Donnie asked as he shook little Joey.

"Do I look like I'm awake?!" snapped little Joey.

"Well, actually you do", interrupted Bert, little Joey usually slept with his eyes open, which was odd.

"Right then guys, what's the plan now?", asked little Joey, shaking the dirt from his fur and trying to wake up properly.

Bert sat next to him and Donnie sat on the other side of little Joey, as Bert began to start explaining the plan.

"We need to contact Dotty and get him here as soon as possible", Bert said.

"In all honesty, Dotty won't be up and about for a couple of hours", said Big Joey, climbing out of the rabbit hole, not really looking at them.

"What?! Is that little Joey" Big Joey added, his eyesight wasn't as good as it once was, especially in the failing light of day.

"Yes papa, it's me", said little Joey.

"How? When?" said Big Joey, very surprised.

"Last night, Bert and Donnie rescued me from the hutch with the help of Dotty", little Joey said.

"I'm glad you are home, safe again", said Big Joey, giving him a hug, wrapping his huge paws around him.

"So, what are you boys up to?" Big Joey questioned.

"Bert has a new plan, papa, he's just about to explain it", Donnie said.

Chapter 8

NEW FOR OLD PLAN

"New plan? Was there an old one?" big Joey
said.
"Actually, there was an old plan" Bert said,
smugly.
"What's the new idea then Bert?" asked big Joey.
"I was just making changes in my head to the old
plan because we now have little Joey and Dotty
to be included in the new one", said Bert.
"And me, count me in too", big Joey said.
"You?   Erm, are you sure Papa?" asked Bert.

Big Joey hadn't been involved in any caper for
such a long time.
"Yes me!" he boomed, "I want to be involved!!
For some reason, I don't get included these days,
you all probably think I'm too old" added big
Joey.
"No, no papa, we don't think you're too old",
they all said at the same time, having their
fingers crossed behind their backs. They did
think he could slow them down when they
needed to be much quicker.

"Right, back to it" Bert said, getting confused as the new and old plans joined together in his head.

Big Joey, little Joey and Donnie listened carefully so as not to miss anything, even though Bert hadn't even started explaining yet.

"Why are you all sat waiting for me to explain?" asked Bert, "has anyone contacted Dotty yet?"

From above them, they heard "look out!" as Dotty swooped in. "Who contacted you?" asked Bert.

"You know, Tony" said Dotty, with a slight wink, mistakenly.

"Tony?" asked big Joey, not too sure if he'd heard Dotty properly.

"I erm, I said 'you know me'", Dotty replied, stumbling over his words.

Big Joey looked at Dotty, not really convinced with what he had said, when he was sure that he'd heard something different.

"What are you doing here big Joey?" asked Dotty.

"I told them I wanted to be included in Bert's plan because I haven't been part of any excitement in a long while", replied big Joey.

"Ahhh, I know what you mean", said Dotty, quite excited at the thought of the adventure, "have we started yet?".
"No", said Bert, "we were going to contact you and then start the planning of the heist, hopefully, we will all come up with different ideas that we can smooth out to make a perfect plan", he continued.

"Initially, we were going to do the same as we did when we rescued little Joey from the hutch", said Bert, "but after meeting Snuggles and nearly been eaten" Donnie interrupted, shaking at the mere thought.
"Yes, quite", Dotty agreed, "that's why you want to change the plan then Bert", said Dotty
"You're right Dotty, this is where you come in", Bert said.
"Remember last night when you carried us from Gregory's garden?", asked Bert, not really needing Dotty to answer, "well, it was much quicker and less dangerous than climbing the walls of the carrot farm or going along the bramble bushes again".

"One problem I see", said Dotty, "big Joey is now part of this great heist".

"I see what you mean Dotty", "and it would mean more work for you but if you don't mind", said Bert

"If I don't mind what?", said Dotty

"If you don't mind the extra journey that is", Bert replied.

"Of course not", Dotty said, smiling with even more excitement, letting out a hoot of delight.

"Okay then, the idea would be to drop us, me, little Joey and Donnie, as close to the cheese factory as possible without being seen, then come back for big Joey", Bert said, quite relaxed, "we will wait for you and big Joey to arrive, then continue with the rest of the plan from there", he added.

"The rest of the plan? And what is that exactly", wondered little Joey.

"I'm not really so sure, but you can help me on this" Bert said, looking hopeful.

"I do know this, Dotty will be waiting to bring the Gorgonzola back to the rabbit hole so that we can divide it up.   Some for me and the rest we may be able to trade with the mice that live in other parts of the corn field and around carrot farm", said Bert.

"Sounds good so far", Dotty said, giving Bert a supportive twist of his head.

Owls couldn't nod very well, so a twist of the head was just as good.

"If we are as close to the factory as possible, we will still have a little way to go, otherwise, we will be seen.   Then we can get onto the trolley with the churns on and wait for someone to take the trolley in", little Joey said, "me, Papa and Donnie may have to hide in open, empty churns until we're inside the door, because we are too big to hide around the churns, but we will have to see nearer the time".

"What a good idea", said Bert.

"Once inside, we need to get from the milk area into the cheese fermentation storage, where all the cheese is stored", little Joey continued.

"How do we get the cheese outside?" Dotty asked.

"There's an old piece of air conditioning pipe that runs to the car park at the back of the factory, we could roll the Gorgonzola down that and into a sack that we will have to put on the pipe before we get on to the churn trolley", little Joey answered, "I will tie the sack onto the pipe as I'm the quickest of us all when it comes to hopping speeds".

Little Joey was the national champion in the annual 100 metres rabbit run, three years unbeaten, which didn't help when Gregory captured him.

"Where is this sack you talk about?" asked Donnie, "we don't have any sacks in the rabbit hole".

"Good point Donnie", little Joey answered, "the factory usually has them scattered around so they can take the cheese to the market to sell, so that shouldn't be a problem".

"Oh, Okay", Donnie replied, somewhat relieved that they didn't have to find a sack too.

"Then I will untie the sack so Dotty can bring it back to the rabbit hole", continued little Joey, "the rest of us will have to make it back on foot".

"On foot?!" big Joey asked, worried that he would slow the group down.

"Yes papa, on foot", replied little Joey, "don't worry, there will be nobody left behind or taken prisoner, I will make sure of that", he said reassuringly.

"How will we make our escape?" asked Bert.

"I was hoping that you would organise that part of the plan because you have been over there more recently when you rescued me", said little

Joey, "besides, I've been locked up for ages and things will have changed around the fields".

"Okay, here's what we need to do then", started Bert, "once we are out of the factory and sure that Dotty is on his way back to the rabbit hole, we make our way down the air conditioning pipe that we rolled the cheese down and through the hedgerow towards the carrot farm", Bert continued.

"Oh no, what about Snuggles?" said Donnie, shaking in his fur again.

"Don't worry about Snuggles, I have dealt with guard dogs before and they aren't fit to guard anything once I've sorted them out", said big Joey, proud of his background as a bare paw boxer in the fields Naples.

He had been a bare paw boxer before he ended up in the Verminage, he started his career very early in life and wanted to do it professionally but injury prevented him from doing so. He'd stood on a hawthorn, putting an end to his dreams there and then.

"So, with Snuggles taken care of, we just have to tackle the wall of the carrot farm again and then we should be home safe", Bert finished smiling, proud of himself.

Even though it was little Joey that had come up with most of the plan.
"It's now too late to get started tonight, we'll have to be ready for the midnight chimes tomorrow", said big Joey and they all nodded, well, all except Dotty, who made a sort of head turning gesture in place of a nod.

Dotty did his usual hop in a circle to take off, flapped his wings and he was up in the air, into the darkness of the night sky. "Cheerio and toodles", he hooted in the distance.
"Right boys, into the rabbit hole", said big Joey, "mama will be so happy you're home little Joey".

Chapter 9

SURPRISE!

Bert scurried down the rabbit hole first, followed by Donnie, big Joey and finally little Joey, hopping into the family home.

Mama was stood near the sink in the kitchen, starting to make a dish of carrot casserole and a fresh batch of cornjack.

"Hey beautiful", big Joey said, putting his paws over Mama Albino's eyes, "I've got a surprise for you"

"Knock it off, you silly bunny!" Mama shrieked, "you made me jump".

Little Joey walked into the kitchen with Donnie and Bert, he stood in front of Mama as big Joey removed his paws from her eyes.

"Surprise!" exclaimed big Joey.

She opened her eyes slowly, not really knowing what to expect, she was expecting some gift for the kitchen that big Joey would normally bring. It wasn't usual for Mama to get anything nice for herself.

Looking through the blur of her recently opened eyes, Mama saw a tall, slim rabbit.

"Little Joey? Is that you?" Mama asked with a shaky voice.

"Yes Mama, it's me", answered little Joey.

"My Bambino", she cried, "you look like you have lost weight, it's a good job I'm making fresh carrot casserole", she said, with tears of joy rolling down her face, "did you get released?", Mama asked.

"No Mama, Bert, Donnie and Dotty came to get me out, I'm on the run from the hutch", little Joey said.

"At least you're home safe", Mama sighed, giving him another hug while looking at Bert and Donnie with shock that they hadn't said anything to anyone.

"Enough now Fiorela, we have a big day tomorrow", said big Joey, "you boys get some proper sleep and we'll sit down for family breakfast in the afternoon".

Fiorela was Mama Albino's name but only big Joey was allowed called her by her given name, for everyone else, it was either Mama or Mrs Albino.

"Joey?" Fiorela said, sitting at the table, "what do you mean, 'we have a big day tomorrow', what's going on?".

Big Joey sat down beside her and began to explain, "Bert, little Joey, after they had broken him out of the hutch, and Donnie pieced together a plan, that is little rough around the edges, for a heist at the cheese factory, they asked me and Dotty to help, which we agreed", he said.
Both you and I know that THEY had asked to be included in the plan.
"It all sounds too risky to me", said Fiorela, "and with little Joey recently out of the hutch, I fear for your safety", she added, looking very worried.
"We will be okay Fiorela, little Joey already told us, no matter what, we leave nobody behind", big Joey said, trying to settle her nerves, leaning over to give her a big rabbit hug.
"There's only one thing for it Joey, I'm coming too" Mama said.
"What?! No no!! We need you here to, erm, make the food for when we get home", said big Joey, trying to convince Mama that it would not be safe for her and that they would be okay without her.

They had kept little Joey's room as it was before he was caught. Bert and Donnie shared a room, the rest or should I say most of the other Albino's had their own rabbit holes, scattered around the various fields close by and some were living in the halls of the Verminersity, similar to a university that humans go to.

Little Joey climbed into his size 14 shoe box, pulled the covers over his shoulders and let out a big sigh, "it's nice to be home" he said, drifting off to sleep.   Meanwhile, Bert and Donnie were still excited about the Gorgonzola heist and how soon it was. They obviously couldn't sleep just yet, "Bert" Donnie said, "isn't this exciting and nerve wracking at the same time?!" he squeaked, in a high pitched voice.
"Yes it is but it's also good to have little Joey home too", replied Bert, "now we really must get some sleep, or we'll be very tired when we have to be alert".
"Ok Bert", said Donnie, even though he didn't want to sleep, "night Bert".
"Good night Donnie, if I'm up first, I'll wake you and if you're up first, you wake me?" Bert said.
"Ok Bert, sleep well", Donnie mumbled as he was beginning to snore.

Bert was just staring at the ceiling again, the plan for cheese heist rolling over and over in his mind, he wasn't nervous about tomorrow, he was scared but kept telling himself that everything would be ok and that it would all go smoothly.

The next day, Bert and Donnie were woken by little Joey, "come on you two lazy bones, it's nearly evening time, we still have a fair amount to organise before it gets to midnight and have breakfast with the family".
Midnight was the best time for any heist, people were usually in bed and couldn't be a risk to them.

They both sprung upright in their beds, "it's my cheese, nobody else's" said Bert in a blind panic, trying to clutch at the alarm clock that hadn't sounded. In reality, the alarm hadn't even been set, they didn't even have an alarm clock, he had obviously been dreaming.

Donnie was slowly coming around after hearing Bert scrambling around, he hadn't heard little Joey shout them.
"What time is it Bert?" Donnie asked, showing him his watch.
"It's time to get up", Bert replied.

"Oh, I'm hungry again", said Donnie, rubbing his rumbling stomach.

Chapter 10
SUPPLIES

Little Joey and Bert went to find supplies they needed for the heist while Donnie dragged his lazy fluffy tail out of bed, somewhat blurry eyed and concentrating on the hunger that was beginning to take over every little thought he may have had.

"Bert, what exactly do we need?" asked little Joey

"Well, we need some string, the hook of an old coat hanger" replied Bert, reeling off the list that he and Donnie had used to rescue him.

"Hang on a minute", little Joey interrupted, "isn't that some of the equipment that you had to spring me from the hutch?"

"It is indeed" said Bert, quite proud of his ability to remember things from a couple of days earlier.

"Ok" said little Joey, "you grab all of the stuff you had then and I will look for things that may also be useful for the heist".

Meanwhile, Donnie had just about managed to get to the side of his bed and put his large paws on to the ground of the rabbit hole, scratching his ears roughly, as if he had a whole ants nest running riot in there.

"Donnie!" cried Bert, scurrying into the bedroom, "where's the rucksack we used to get little Joey out of the hutch?"

"Errrrm, it's here somewhere" replied Donnie, scrabbling through a pile of laundry that really needed washing or it would grow legs and take itself to be washed.

"Here it is Bert, it was under last month's socks" said Donnie.

He'd figured that if he used less clothing, Mama wouldn't have so much washing to do and then she would have more time for the cooking, thinking of his stomach once again.

Bert snatched the rucksack and headed back out of the bedroom to look for little Joey after quickly checking the bag to make sure that everything was there and that there weren't any escapees from the dirty laundry pile.

He went through the rabbit hole, every nook and darkened piece of it.

Little Joey had popped out of the rabbit hole to take in some of the refreshing early evening air. Bert eventually checked outside after running out of places to look inside the rabbit hole.
"There you are little Joey" said Bert, "I have looked everywhere for you".
"Did you find the rucksack Bert?" little Joey asked.
"Yes, I did" replied Bert, "long story, one that I would rather not re-live, what did you find?"
Little Joey took a deep breath as if to reel off a huge list of items and simply replied "it's all in the back of the store hole", having a chuckle to himself.

The pair went back into the rabbit hole and made their way towards the kitchen for the family breakfast that they had planned the night before. Mama was in the kitchen, warming up leftover carrots, Donnie was, of course, already sat at the table, paws at the ready, drooling at the thought of carrots for breakfast. Carrots as a main meal were quite a normal dish but carrots for breakfast, well, that was for posh rabbits.
Just as Bert and little Joey reached the table to sit down, big Joey came stumbling through the door, looking like he didn't have a clue where he was, or even who he was.

"Joey!" Mama shouted at big Joey, "have you washed your paws and behind your ears?"
"Of course, Fiorela" big Joey replied, winking at the others.
"Ok Joey, how much of this fried carrot and lettuce omelette do you want?" she asked.

Now, having carrots for breakfast was indeed a luxury but to have lettuce too, well that was very exciting, although, to call it an omelette when it didn't even contain any eggs was a little far fetch.   It was both the carrot and lettuce, squashed together, using a bit of old potato to make sure it stuck together rather than looking mashed up and unappealing.
"Just give me a little to start with please Fiorela, the boys need to keep their energy up and if there's seconds, I'll have some more", he responded with a knowing smile.   Knowing that she would have made more than enough for thirds let alone seconds.

A quick glance around the table at her boys, Mama was so proud yet worried at the same time, as she knew that tonight's heist could go either way. On one hand, it could go so smoothly that a silk worm would be happy with the result or so badly that she would NEVER see any of them again.

Chapter 11

LETTUCE PRAY

"Has everyone got their breakfast?" asked big Joey.

All of them nodding as they tucked in without even thanking the Supreme Rabbit.

The Supreme Rabbit wasn't like a god or anything like, he was the oldest rabbit in the field, that they would thank for each important meal, by saying a few words before eating. "Donnie! Take that out of your paws this very minute" big Joey boomed as Donnie nearly choked on what he had already got in his mouth. Big Joey place both paws together and bowed his head in thought. "Lettuce Pray", he said, making a little joke to lighten the mood, "We thank you Supreme Rabbit, for the bounty that you have granted us from the fields", Joey started.

While Donnie was trying to stuff his face with the odd paw full of food, so that he could get more before anyone else had their paws on it.

Big Joey continued the thanks until he reached the end, with a shake of his fluffy tail by way of finishing the long and usually boring speech. "That was lovely Joey", said Mama, while the rest of them just tucked into their food, not really concerned with giving thanks, they would have had to collect the carrots and lettuce from the nearby fields themselves anyway. Obviously thinking that they earned it and not actually grateful to the Supreme Rabbit.

It was because of the Supreme Rabbit and his Supreme Burrowers, that the crops even existed in the first place.

The Supreme Burrowers were a large group of elder rabbits that specialised in growing the crops just for the rabbits so none of them would see the wrong end of the farmer's gun because they had stolen his crops instead.
There had been a lot of poor rabbits that had seen the wrong end of the farmer's gun but only the Supreme Rabbit lived to tell the story.

Donnie had almost finished his plate and planning thirds before even being asked if he wanted seconds, the rest of them hadn't even started eating yet.

After an hour, several seconds and third helpings later, they had all finished eating. "Right!" said big Joey, "who's washing the plates?" as he looked around to see four empty chairs, even Mama had vanished from the kitchen. "Looks like I'm washing up then", he mumbled to himself. He didn't really mind but once in a while it would have been nice if one of the boys actually did chores instead of leaving it to him and Mama.

After he had washed all the plates, big Joey walked through the rabbit hole to go outside, so he could smoke his favourite pipe.
He didn't smoke it often but when the need for deep thought came, it was pipe smoking time and tonight's plan would need lots of deep thought, with the heist laying heavily on his mind.
A pipe was quite an unusual object for any rabbit to have, but his was made from a hollowed out acorn for the bowl, a bit of twig that woodworm had eaten a hole through it and was held together with old, used chewing gum that had been thrown over the wall of the wheat field, but it was HIS pipe and that made him happy.

As big Joey reached the opening of the rabbit hole, he heard little Joey, Donnie, Bert and Mama talking about the Gorgonzola Heist and a little bit of what they had planned so far, trying to put Mama's mind at rest.

Chapter 12
WAITING FOR DOTTY

"It's ok, you can go back in now, the plates have been washed" big Joey said, with a little smile breaking through the seriousness of his voice. "We are waiting for Dotty to arrive", said Bert even though it hadn't even started to become dark yet. Bert was clearly very excited to get his plan underway, "have we got everything we need?" asked Bert, looking at little Joey for support or at least a sign that he was listening. As with most Rabbits, little joey's attention span was limited to a few seconds.
"Everything?" questioned little Joey.
"Yes, everything!" exclaimed Bert.
"You have the rucksack and the equipment that you used to spring me from the hutch at Gregory's and I got a few other things that I think will help this heist go smoothly and more importantly, safely" replied little Joey with a smug grin on his face.

There was a big sigh of relief from Bert and a relaxed look on everyone else's face, including

Mama.

She was worrying for all of them and hoping
that they would all return safely.

As they all hugged Mama reassuringly, one by
one, big Joey spoke "I think I can hear Dotty, but
it isn't even dark yet".

"I told you we were waiting for him" said Bert,
"maybe he is arriving early to go through the
plan and get his part firmly in mind".

Just as Bert had finished speaking, Dotty's
shadow was covering all of them as he came into
land.

"Good evening" Dotty said, as he folded up his
large wings.

"You're early" said Donnie, who had been
listening to Bert and little Joey talking.

"My dear boy, I am not early, merely not late"
Dotty chuckled at his own intellect.

"I will leave you boys to get organised for night
fall and go tidy up the kitchen from breakfast,
see you boys in the morning" said Mama as she
climbed back down the rabbit hole.

Chapter 13

THE PLAN UNFOLDED

"Ok, who wants to start this meeting" said Bert looking around for enthusiasm.

"It is your idea, isn't it Bert?" little Joey said.

"Well, yes, ok I guess I should start it then?" Bert replied, in a sort of questioning manner as everyone else nodded their heads in agreement.

"Right then, here goes. We will make our way to Gregory's as Donnie and I did to rescue little Joey" Bert started, "Once in the garden we will use the hutch to assist climbing into the yard of the cheese factory as Dotty watches from above so he can alert us of any dangers that are close by" continued Bert.

"So, I'm not airlifting you all now?" asked Dotty.

"It's too much to ask of you" said big Joey.

"Ok" replied Dotty, "how will I alert you exactly Bert?", knowing that they didn't have any walkie-talkies, allowing them to talk to each other.

"Dotty, if you give us one hoot to let us know that there is danger close by, two hoots if the coast is clear and a long hoot if we need to run like the wind and avoid being caught or worse, eaten!" replied Bert.

"That's seems straight forward" said Dotty, "please continue Bert".

"Where was I?   Ah yes, once over the wall into the yard of the factory, we will use the shadows to hide ourselves as we make our way up to the area where the churns are kept and wait for a human to take us inside the factory.   There, we will take our positions" continued Bert once again.

"Our positions?" questioned big Joey.

"Yes" answered Bert.

"And, what exactly are those positions Bert?" big Joey asked.

"I haven't quite figured the roles out yet Papa but" he replied, as little Joey interrupted.

"Bert, you find the cheese store, as your nose is more likely to find it than ours, Donnie, you keep a look out, humans might try to squash him" said little Joey as Bert gave a big GULP sound at the thought of being squashed.

"Papa, you make sure that Donnie is keeping alert and tell him when it is safe for him to go into the cheese store after Bert, you follow him and I will be the last in" little Joey said as the rest listened intently.

"I thought of that" said Bert, knowing full well, he hadn't really thought of much with regards to roles during the heist, with very little but cheese on his mind.   "Once in the cheese store, I will find the best cheese, ones that have matured to the correct smelliness" Bert continued.

"Is everyone ready to go now?" asked Bert. They all looked around and appeared to agree that they were ready to leave but suddenly

Donnie looked a little nervous, "I need the toilet" he said, "I'll be quick" and off he hopped to the nearest part of the hedgerow.

"Anyone else need to go?" asked Bert getting somewhat agitated by now.

"No, just Donnie, you know how he is when he is really nervous Bert" replied big Joey as Donnie hopped back to the group.

"Let's get going" said Bert, eager to get his plan finally started.

The group set off, along the hedgerow and Brambles, towards the wall of the carrot farm and towards Snuggles, with great hops and scurries as Dotty took off skywards, in his usual circling manner.

Bert thought to himself, 'It was a great relief that Dotty was circling about them'.

"Shhhh!" said little Joey.

Bert was thinking aloud again.

"Did I just say that out loud?" Bert asked.

"Yes" little Joey replied, "We are supposed to be keeping a low profile".

As they neared the wall, big Joey gave the signal to stop and prepare to climb, which, for any rabbit, having such small front legs and paws, was a task in itself.

He took off the rucksack that he was given to carry and opened it.

"Sandwiches?!" he exclaimed, "Who brought sandwiches?"

The group look at one another blankly as if they were mutely saying, 'they are not mine!', then it came to him, Mama would have made them for the journey or the return journey as they could be out of the rabbit hole for some time.

"Oh, it must have been Mama!" he said, "Looking after us all, as usual" he continued, humbly.

After carefully taking out the sandwiches and placing them gently on a nearby tree stump, he took out the hook of the old coat hanger, with the string still attached, passed it to Donnie to throw.
"Go on Donnie, you're the expert on this" he said with a little wink.
"I'm no expert" responded Donnie, his face lighting up that someone even thought of him as an expert.
"Well, you have done this at least once before, I have NEVER done this, so, that makes you an expert" big Joey said, putting the hook and string firmly into the paws of Donnie.

Donnie took a hop back, did a sort of bodily twisting motion, unravelled the string a little and SWOOSH! went the string, coming back as quickly as he had thrown it.   He had thrown the wrong end.
"Take your time" said Bert reassuringly.

Donnie took hold of the hook this time, repeated the hop back and body twisting motion, almost bending himself out of his round rabbit shape and threw the hook as hard as he could, with a dull CLUNK noise, the hook grasped the top of the wall. 'It actually landed first time this time' thought Bert as Donnie just turned and stared at him intcnscly.

He was thinking aloud yet again, now with an increasingly embarrassed expression.

Donnie gave the string a firm pull to make sure it was secure before anyone could climb it, turned around and asked "Who's first?", looking at the rest of them.

"Bert" said little Joey, "After all, it is his plan and he can remember some of his training from the Mouse Brigade"

Bert reluctantly stepped forward, taking hold of the string using the method he had used previously and began to climb the wall of the carrot farm, occasionally catching a glimpse of Dotty circling above them all.

Once he had reached the top, he pulled the string so whoever was to climb next, knew that he wasn't still climbing.

"Right Papa, you go next, then Donnie, I will climb last" said little Joey.
Big Joey had already grabbed the string before little Joey had even said anything, he just wanted to get the climb over with, he was quite unfit after years of doing very little activity, combined with Mama's home cooking.

Big Joey began to climb up the wall, trying to use the technique that he watch Bert use but unsuccessfully, he quickly thought back to his days in the Verminage and physical education classes that were taught there.
In no time at all, he was at the top, wheezing like a broken Acordion but happy that he hadn't fallen off the string at any point.

He shook the string for Donnie to start climbing but as usual, Donnie was complaining about being hungry after seeing little Joey pack the sandwiches back into the rucksack.
"Go on Donnie, we need to get over this wall before we even think about food" said little Joey, putting on the rucksack in readiness for the climb.

Donnie took hold of the string and up he went, quickly getting out of breath.   He was more unfit than Papa was.

After some time, around fifteen minutes, Donnie had made it to the top, helped up by big Joey. He gave the string a little shake and collapsed on top of the wall, trying to stop his heart from jumping out of his chest and breathing with the noise of a steam train.

Little Joey quickly looked around after hearing a rustle in the Bramble bushes but couldn't see anything.   Thankfully my clumsy footing didn't give my location away, I had climbed the bushes so that I could see and hear what was going on.

Little Joey began to climb the string to the top of the wall, when the hook started to become loose, he paused for a few moments until the string had stopped moving and the hook had settled back into a safe position, then continued his climb, until he had reached the others.
At the top, they waited until everyone had stopped panting like a dog that had been running for days.

"Can we eat yet?" asked Donnie.

"Not just yet my boy, just a little further, then we will eat" replied big Joey.

"Hoot!" came the noise from above them, they had to wait, Dotty came to land on top of the wall to give them a progress report. He was quite adept at these sorts of missions.

"Well done everyone!" he said, "I gave the one hoot signal as I had noticed Snuggles laying near the door of the storage shed, in the shadows, chained of course but we all know that chain reaches the boundaries of the carrot farm".

Little Joey moved the hook to the opposite side of the wall so that they could climb down as soon as it was safe to.

"So far, we have done quite well" said Bert, in agreement with Dotty, "But this is where it gets dangerous".

As he had finished talking, big Joey nudged him and pointed in the direction of the storage shed, Snuggles was going in, assumedly to get his night feed.

"Now is our chance" he said, "We will climb down in the same order we climbed up"

Bert took hold of the string and started to lean
back, another technique he had learned in the
Mouse Brigade, although rarely used it.
Within seconds he was on the ground, inside the
carrot farm wall.

Dotty flapped his huge wings, going into the
blackness of the night sky, to watch for danger.

Chapter 14

FRIEND OR FOE

As big Joey climbed down the string, the only way he knew how, slowly, there was a clanging noise coming from the storage shed.
It was Snuggles, he was knocking his metal food bowl about trying, unsuccessfully, to get the last morsels of his food.
"Hurry!" whispered Bert, "Snuggles is finishing his food!!"

Big Joey, slid down the string, as quickly as he could and reached the ground next to Bert.
"Donnie!   I am down" he shouted in a whisper.
Donnie started his climb down the string as the hook began to move slightly, then jolt suddenly, making Donnie slide down the string, at an alarming rate of speed.   THUD!!
"OUCH!" Donnie and big Joey both exclaimed as he had fallen a little way down the string and landed directly on top of Papa.
"This isn't the time for messing around!" said Bert, trying to listen for other noises coming from the shed.

"Little Joey, we are clear of the string" said big Joey, a little louder than before.

An almighty CRASH! Came out of the storage shed, Snuggles must have knocked something over and fearing he would be in trouble from his master, ventured out into the night air, with an 'It was not me' kind of walk.
"HOOOOO!!" Dotty was shouting from above, "HOOOOOOO!!" he exclaimed again, not knowing if they could hear him.
Little Joey was only halfway down the wall when Snuggles spotted them next to the wall.

He sprang into action, "Friend or Foe?" he snarled.
To which Donnie replied with a question, "What is a Foe?"
Snuggles looked quite shocked, he had never had to explain it before but tried the best he could.
"Well, it is the opposite of friend" he started.
"What? An unfriend?" Donnie asked, quite confused.
"Wait a treat eating minute" exclaimed Snuggles, "don't I know you from somewhere?"

"Erm, No?!" replied Donnie trying to hide the fact that they had escaped him before.

"Yeah, I DO know you!" said Snuggles with a menacing look on his face, "you were here a few nights ago and I was going to ask you, who you are, then a huge owl came and carried you off. I thought you were as dead as a coffin nail"

"You would have eaten us anyway, if the owl hadn't carried us off" said Bert.

Big Joey was readying himself to punch Snuggles straight on the nose if he got any closer.

"You got me all wrong" said Snuggles, "this is just an act for my master, I don't even like the taste of mice or rabbit, but sadly, my master made me try it, I became sick and he never gave me it again.   These days I just eat vegetables, they taste nice and I don't get sick"

"So you weren't going to eat us after all?" asked Bert.

"Bow Wow Wow" laughed Snuggles, showing his more enjoyable side, "like I said, it's all an act for my master, you are quite safe"

Little Joey reached the bottom of the wall and was quite surprised at what confronted his eyes.

"It's ok Snuggles, he is with us" said Donnie.

"How do you know my name?" Snuggles asked

"We have heard your master calling you" replied big Joey, "I am big Joey, these are my boys, little Joey, Donnie, Bert, and the owl is Godfrey Brown but we call him Dotty, on account of his feathers"

"Nice to meet you all, it's not often you get anyone visiting the carrot farm that doesn't run away from me" said Snuggles sadly, "My full name is Snugglesby Percy but my master just shouts Snuggles all the time"

"Right boys, we have to get a move on" said big Joey.

"A move on?" asked Snuggles

"Yes" answered Bert, "I have thought about this moment for some time and we now have a plan for a heist at the cheese factory"

"I would love to help but my chain only goes as far as Gregory's garden wall" said Snuggles sadly.

"Oh, but you can help dear boy!" said Dotty as he flew into land, after realising that Snuggles was a friend and not a foe.

"What?! How?" asked Snuggles, somewhat surprised at Dotty's remark, "I can only go as far as that wall", looking in the direction of Gregory's garden and raising a paw in a pointing manner.

Most dogs couldn't actually point, unless they were a Pointer and they were very good at pointing, because they stared at what they were looking at, in an almost crazed way. Snuggles' version of pointing was more of a limp wristed attempt.
"You can reach the top of the wall if you stand at full length" insisted Dotty.
"Well, yes, my paws will reach to the top and over it, on some parts of the wall" said Snuggles, a little confused as to how that would be helping.
"Right then" continued Dotty, "if you stand as you would, looking over the wall, Bert, little Joey, Donnie and big Joey can climb up your back and onto the wall, then drop the string down the other side to climb down".
"What a great idea Dotty" said big Joey.

Before anyone had a chance to say anything else, Snuggles had already made his way towards the wall and was stood up, with his paws hooked over the top of the wall.

Little Joey gave the string a shake and side stepped as the coat hanger hook came loose, falling to the ground.

"Bert, gather up the string and hook, then meet us over at the wall with Snuggles" said little Joey, as he set off towards the rest of them at the wall.

Bert quickly gathered up the string and hook as he watched the rest of them disappear into the darkness of the carrot farm towards Gregory's garden wall, with the occasional glimpse of moonlight through the clouds or the security lights that came on long enough to see what they needed to see before plunging them back into darkness, waiting for their eyes to adjust and almost forgetting which way they needed to go.

Dotty opened his wings to take flight once more and "FLAP!!" was the noise he made as he almost knocked Bert over with the force of the wind he had made with them, "FLAP!!" went the noise again.

It wasn't a noise of air passing through his feathers, it was the noise that he made with his beak, just for effect.

"I'm here" said Bert, looking for a sign that they may have missed him, but they had only been gone for a minute.

"We were waiting for you" said Donnie, with a sound of desperate hunger in his voice.

"I'm staaaaarrrrrvvvvv…" he started to speak again.

"Stop right there Donnie!" snapped big Joey, working out what Donnie was about to say.

"It's only been about 50 minutes since you last ate something you'll have to wait until later to quieten that stomach of yours".

Chapter 15

GREGORY'S WALL

With Snuggles in position, waiting for the next stage of his role in the plan, as keen to please them, as he was his master.

"Who's first?" asked little Joey.

"I'll go first, after all, I still have the hook and string for the climb down" replied Bert, as he readied himself to climb onto the back of Snuggles.

"Ok then Bert, you go first, Donnie can go next, followed by Papa then I will follow behind" said little Joey.

Bert scampered up the hind leg of Snuggles, quickly over his back and shoulders, then a little jump onto the top of the wall.

"I'm up!" shouted Bert, as they all stood watching from below.

Donnie was next to go, tripping over his own paws in the rush to climb Snuggles' back, so much so, that he slipped off a couple of times to the frustration of Bert, who was waiting for Donnie to help him unravel the hook and string, that had become tangled whilst climbing Snuggles' back.

Eventually, Donnie reached the top of the wall, helped Bert unravel the string.
Bert handed him the end of the string and threw the hook onto the ground, then hit himself in the face with his paw after realising that he had thrown down the wrong end.
Big Joey arrived at the top, closely followed by little Joey.
"All set Bert?" questioned little Joey as Bert was still pulling up the hook from when he had thrown it.
"Erm… Nearly, I accidently threw the hook down instead of the end of the string which I gave to Donnie" replied Bert, a little confused with himself.

Finally, Bert had all the string gathered up and hook in paw. He hooked it on to the top of the wall and gave it a firm pull to make sure that it wasn't going to move.
"Right Little Joey, it's all set to go now" Bert exclaimed, with a slightly happier face than he had a few minutes before.
"Right Bert" said little Joey, "same order as last time".

"Good luck boys!" said Snuggles "I'm going back to actually finish my evening feed, give me a shout if you need any more help on this side of the wall".

"Thank you Snuggles" they replied.

Well, all, except Donnie who was trying to silence his stomach before the climb down and hadn't even noticed that Snuggles had gone.

"Donnie!" shouted little and big Joey together,

"What?!" snapped Donnie

"It's your turn to get down the string into the cheese factory yard" said little Joey

"I thought Bert was going first" replied Donnie

"He has, he's been waiting for you to climb down for 10 minutes, while you were rubbing your growling stomach" said big Joey.

With that, Donnie took hold of the string and headed down the wall, now abseiling like a professional.

Within seconds, he was at the bottom of the wall, looking smugly at Bert, even though he hadn't been any quicker than Bert, it was quite an achievement for Donnie.

Big Joey came flying down the string, almost knocking the smile from Donnie's face, he didn't quite taken hold of the string before he left the top of the wall.

Little Joey came next, trying to loosen the hook from the top of the wall before heading on to the next stage of the heist.

"Leave it little Joey" said Bert, "we have a different escape route planned, don't we?!"

"Yeah! But…" little Joey was about to finish the sentence when he was interrupted by Papa,

"leave it!!" he said, sounding somewhat angry, but as they all knew, it was his way of getting his point across.

With that, little Joey left the hook and string where it was, summoning the rest of the group to a small 'next step' meeting, a sort of refresher as to what was going to be happening next.

"You and Donnie find the next batch of milk churns to be taken into the factory" said little Joey, staring straight at Bert, who seemed to be in a bit of a cheese hypnosis, at the thought of what is going to happen in the next step of this escapade.

"Bert?" little Joey said, "are you actually listening?"

"Cheese!" exclaimed Bert, coming out of his trance like state. "Erm, I mean, of course I'm listening, Donnie and I have to go to the milk churns and find the next one to be taken in".

"I thought you weren't listening" said little Joey

"I wasn't" mumbled Bert whilst nudging Donnie and winking.

Well, sort of winking, it looked more like he had a whisker in his eye.

"Oh yeah" said Donnie, not really paying attention either, he was too busy nursing his growling stomach and thinking of carrot casserole, topped off with cabbage sundae for dessert.

"me and Papa will follow you, but not too closely" said little Joey

"Why not too closely?" asked Donnie, "we don't smell!"

"Hoo Hoo Hoo!" came the sound of a laughing Dotty above them, having heard a little of the conversation.

"I didn't mean that you smell, I meant that we could also keep a lookout from behind" said little Joey "if things were to go wrong, there wouldn't be anyone left to form a rescue party except Dotty and he isn't able to be of much use on the ground".

"Ah! I see now" said Donnie, "come on Bert, lets crack on before it gets to daytime again" With that, Bert and Donnie headed towards the factory churn store, almost on tip-toes, so they wouldn't be heard, followed by big and little Joey, all under the watchful eye of Dotty.

The churn store was a dark damp area at the side of the factory, it wasn't used much in the summer because the milk would go off too quickly and then it would be pointless trying to make cheese from it, they may as well just add some fruit and call it yoghurt!

Bert stopped suddenly, almost frozen to the spot, a huge shadow had appeared at his feet.
"What's wrong Bert" asked Donnie.
"There is someone behind us" said Bert, afraid to look back.
"It's Papa and little Joey" said Donnie, taking a quick look.
"They are rabbits and this shadow is mouse shaped" said Bert, his voice trembling slightly.
"Bert, there is nobody else behind us, hang on a minute, Gregory has turned his light on" said Donnie

Bert breathed a very large sigh of relief as he realised that whoever it was behind them, wasn't actually behind them at all, in fact, there was nobody as Donnie had said, it was his own shadow.

"It's ok Donnie, forget I ever said anything" said Bert, a little embarrassed.

As they approached the churn store, Bert gave the signal that it was all clear, both little Joey and big Joey could now follow them at a closer distance.

Bert and Donnie, saw a wide opening in the wall, that had been created by a large family of rats that lived there, long before it became a cheese factory.

Bert and Donnie went inside, "I'll wait here for little Joey and Papa" said Donnie, quite scared of the dark, damp and strange surroundings, waiting for his eyes to adjust properly.

Donnie was waiting near the hole, so that big and little Joey knew where they had gone, occasionally sticking out his paw and waiving it around like a soggy biscuit that had been over-dunked.

Big Joey and little Joey quickly reached the hole in the wall and hopped through, into the same pitch darkness that had surprised Bert and Donnie.

"I found the perfect transport, a churn cart" said Bert, "it's right next to the door into the cheese factory"

Scampering and hopping through the gloom of the churn store, they could just make out the shape of the cart and the numerous churns that were on it.

As they reached the churn cart, Bert climb on board, followed by Donnie, little Joey and finally big Joey, who was out of breath after frantic hopping to get onto the cart.

As they all took positions, to hide themselves from the humans that worked in the factory, the door to the churn store swung open.

Chapter 16
IN THE FACTORY

In through the door came a man the size of a house, well, he could have been that big to a mouse or a rabbit, they didn't see humans too often, except the farmer in the wheat field on the odd occasion.

The man took hold of the handle on the churn cart and proceeded to drag the cart through the door from which he had appeared.
Bert, Donnie, little Joey and big Joey lay in hiding until the cart finally stopped in a line of other carts waiting to be processed.
"Now's our chance" said Bert, readying himself to jump off the cart, "let's go".

Bert swiftly jumped from the cart and into the shadows of a nearby table, quickly followed by the rest.
"that went surprisingly well" said big Joey, proudly, his boys had achieved something quite remarkable.
"we're not out of the woods yet" said little Joey.

This wasn't a great phrase to use around Donnie, you could see his expression looking a bit dumbfounded at what little Joey had just said.

"But" said Donnie, "we're not in the woods, we're in a cheese factory"

Little Joey couldn't be bothered trying to explain it, just looked at Donnie blankly until Donnie realised that he was meaning that they weren't yet safe.

"Now, we have to find the cheese store and the quickest route to it" said little Joey, pulling out a map of the factory.

"where did you get it" said Bert, "it's the first time I've seen that!"

"Ah, a Rabbit has to have some secrets Bert" said little Joey, giving a little wink.

"right, if we carry on walking under this table and around the back of the sink area, we won't be far from the cheese store" said little Joey pointing it out on the map before putting it back under his fur.

As they hopped and scurried under the tables towards the wash area, something didn't feel right to Bert, "Wait" he said.

They all stopped and looked at Bert.

"What is it?" said Donnie.

"I have a bad feeling about this" said Bert.

"well, there isn't much we can do about that now, you should have gone to the toilet before we set off" said big Joey almost chuckling to himself
"not that kind of bad feeling Papa, it's something else that I can't quite put my paw on" said Bert, "forget it, let's just carry on"

They continued passed the sink, under and over all the drainage pipes, heading towards the corner of the room, still out of sight of the humans.

As they reached the corner, they realise that it didn't go around the wall as the map had suggested but was a blocked end to the route.
"told you I had a bad feeling" said Bert looking at them all.
"we'll have to go back" said Joey, looking at the map once more after pulling it from under his fur, "there, just before the sink, we can get across there and we would be much closer to the cheese store".
"But, that looks really risky" said big Joey
"I agree" said Bert.
"There is no other way" said little Joey, "we have to go that way or we could just go home and put this night down to experience".

"what?! No!" said Bert, "we'll give it a try and hopefully remain unseen"

They turned around in the limited space, headed towards the wash area, back over the drainage pipes they went and waited under the table next to the wash area, waiting for what seemed months, for a chance to cross the room without being seen by any of the humans that could pass by at any time.
"Now!" screeched Bert, pushing Donnie out from under the table.

Donnie stopped for a moment then quickly gathered his thoughts and baggy fur, hopping frantically towards, then under the table at the other side of the room, just as a human was passing by.
"little Joey, you go next then Papa and I will be last" said Bert.

With that, little Joey hopped to the table where Donnie was and then big Joey did the same, giving Bert a "paws up" gesture that they had made it to safety, not quite a 'thumbs up', as Rabbits don't have thumbs.

Bert quickly scampered out towards the others
and just as quick, scampered back.
He was almost seen by a human!
"looks like we got rats again" said one of the
men, appearing to talk into thin air, "I'm going
to feel around and see what I can find"
He knelt down and fumbled around under the
table, missing Bert by inches but this was too
close for Bert, dodging the man's fingers at
every sweep.

Bert had dodged one too many times and was
soon in the man's hand, struggling to get free, he
had even tried biting, but couldn't get loose.
The man stood up with Bert in hand, "got the
little fella, aww, it's a little mouse" he said,
"now to get rid of him".

He lay Bert on the table, gripped firmly in his
left hand and reaching for the poison tray with
his right.   Bert, all the while, struggling to free
himself as the others watched helplessly from
under the other table.
As the man slowly brought the poison tray closer
to Bert, the tray getting bigger and bigger in
Bert's view, he could look no more, closed his
eyes, waiting for the tray and almost certain
death, to come.

Instead, he heard a loud slapping noise and the man's hold was no longer there.

As Bert opened his eyes, not knowing what to expect, he didn't notice the man at first and then he saw him, on the floor, a little shaken and behind him was, what appeared to be, a large mouse, running towards the table where the others were.

Bert got back on to his paws, shook his head, ran and jumped from the edge of the table, bouncing off the man's head as he was just picking himself up from the floor and quickly scurried under the table to the others before the man could realise which way he went.

"I don't know what just happened" said Bert, "but I'm sure glad it did".

"This rat saved your life" said Donnie, pointing at the stranger.

"allow me to introduce myself" said the Rat, "my name is Tony, Tony the…"

Just then, big Joey stepped towards the stranger, looked at him closely before saying "Tony 'the Rat' Gambino?"

"yes, the one and only" said Tony.

"Really?!" exclaimed big Joey

"yes, Joey, it's been a while hasn't it" said Tony.

"My old friend" said big Joey, "it's been way too long"

"Me and Tony go very long way back" explained big Joey to the others, "we grew up in the Verminage, we were like brothers"

"What are we waiting for!" said Bert, "we still have a long way to go to get this job done"

"Bert's right, we need to get this done and you guys can catch up back at the rabbit hole" said little Joey.

"I guess I'm part of this job now" said Tony, a little unsure of how they would react.

"Come on Tony" said big Joey, "you saved Bert, of course you're involved".

Little Joey was looking at the map of the factory again, trying to work out the best way to go now. "if we go this way, behind these tables, the store room door is just on the right at the end" said little Joey, "I'll lead the way and Bert can follow behind, everyone else goes in between us"

"Ok" said Donnie, "can I go first?"

"weren't you listening Donnie?!" said Bert, "do we have to repeat everything?"

"No Bert, but my stomach was talking and I have to listen when it speaks" said Donnie.

"well, little Joey is leading the way and I'm at the back of us all, everybody else is in the middle of us" said Bert, "that includes YOU!".

Little Joey tucked the map back under his fur and gave the signal to move, which was a Rabbit thump on the concrete floor, then set off, around the wall under the tables.
"There's a machine up here and it's loud, so we won't be able to hear each other, then we have another table to go under before we reach the end of the wall" said little Joey, almost muffled by the machinery in the distance.
"not that we're talking much now" mumbled Donnie, "and I'm sooooo hungry!".

Chapter 17
THE CHEESE STORE

Walking passed the noisy machine, all with paws covering their ears and Bert almost tripping over the wiring that lay on the floor, they reached the last table.

Little Joey stopped, "this is the last bit of cover before we have another tricky part" said little Joey, "at the end of this table, we will have to go right and wait for the door opening to get into the cheese store"

"once the door is open" said big Joey, "we just make a run for it?".

"exactly that papa, we run like the wind" said little Joey.

"who's got wind?" said Donnie.

"I don't know" said Bert, "it wasn't me.

"nobody has wind" said Tony, "we have to run really, really fast".

"so, where does wind come into it?" asked Donnie, again, very confused.

"forget it Donnie", said little Joey, "it's just a saying".

As they reached the end of the wall, under the table, little Joey looked around the corner towards the cheese store door.

"we're in luck, the door has been left open and we just need to get in there, without been seen" little Joey said.

"I think we should watch for a while" said Tony, "and then we know how often the humans pass, we don't want anyone getting caught, especially as we are so close to what you've set out to do".

"Eye spy with my little eye" said Bert, hoping they could get a quick game in, while they waited.

"We don't have time for that Bert" said Donnie, "We have to watch for humans".

Everyone turned and looked at Donnie, this was the most sense he had made in days.

They all took turns in watching, this could take quite some time and there was no turning back now.   Humans passed quite often at first, then they heard a bell in the distance and suddenly, the humans stopped passing, the factory was as quiet as a mouse, well, most mice except Bert.

"little Joey, I think we're good to go" said Tony, "haven't seen any humans in ages".

They quickly ran towards the cheese store, keeping a lookout all the way, there was no order in who went first or last, they were like a flock of sheep, running aimlessly towards the opening of the door.

Finally, they were inside the cheese store, the strong smell of month old socks filled the air, a mouse's favourite smell.

"Pew!! What's that stink?" asked Donnie, his nose twitching like it was on fire.

"That, my boy, is the smell of the old days" said Tony.

"Smells like old humans if you ask me" said Donnie.

The shelves of the room were stacked full of delicious Gorgonzola, four cheese wheels to a stack and six stacks on every shelf, there must have been over nine hundred cheese wheels in the entire store room, give or take a wheel or two, this was heaven to Bert.

"Bert, how many have we come for?" asked big Joey.

"Erm, well, seeing all this, I have absolutely no idea now" said Bert, his nose moving in the

Gorgonzola filled air, bouncing about like ball on uneven ground, moving in every direction that it could.

"You need to think, and think fast" said Tony, "I don't think those humans will be away for much longer".

With that, Bert looked around to see if there was anything that they could move the cheese with and then remembered that they were going to roll it down the air conditioning pipe, into a bag that Dotty would have hopefully tied on the end.

"I think we'll take two" said Bert.

"Two?!" said little Joey, "that's hardly a Great Gorgonzola Heist, is it?

"Well, what do you suggest then?" asked Bert.

"We need more than that, how else can we trade cheese for carrots or corn for that matter?" said little Joey, "I figure we would get at least four in a bag and there has to be more bags out there".

"Donnie, go find the air conditioning pipe at the back of the store and try talk to Dotty through it" said Tony, "then come back when you know how many bags there are outside".

"Ok" said Donnie.

Into the slightly darker part of the room he went with no question, not even a little moan and had a little smile on his face.

A few moments passed as Donnie reached the pipe that lead out into the carpark at the rear of the factory.

"Psssst! Dotty, are you there?" asked Donnie, whispering down the hole in the wall.

"Hoo" replied Dotty.

"Who? Sorry, I'm trying to speak to Dotty" said Donnie, surprised to think that there could be someone else at the other end of the pipe.

"I said Hoo because I didn't want to make a sound, that owls wouldn't normally do, like a code in case humans heard us" said Dotty, his beak curling up at the edges, trying to hold in a huge laugh.

"Ah!" said Donnie, "how many bags can you see and have you tied one on your end of the pipe?".

"Yes" replied Dotty.

"Yes?" said Donnie, "what do you mean Yes?".

"I mean, yes, I have tied a bag over my end of the pipe" said Dotty.

"and how many are there?" asked Donnie.

"only the one" came Dotty's reply.

"Hang on" said Donnie, "so there's only one bag there and it's on the pipe?".

"There is one on the pipe and about three more close by" said Dotty.

"So, what you are saying is, there are four bags in total?" asked Donnie.

"Yes, but aren't we just using the one" asked Dotty.

"I don't know, they asked me to ask you how many bags there were" said Donnie, "I'm going back to tell them and we should be sending the first wheel out very soon".

"I'll be waiting and keeping watch" said Dotty, unaware that Donnie was hopping his way back to the others and didn't hear the end of what Dotty was saying.

When Donnie arrived back, Tony and big Joey were talking about their days in the Verminage together, what fun times they had, playing tricks on other Rabbits and Rats, not to mention the Hares.

The Hares were in charge of running the Verminage, all dressed in grey cloth, like nuns, very strict too.

"Bert" said Donnie, "there are four bags and one is already tied onto the pipe, Dotty is ready when we are".

"While Donnie was gone, I looked at the

shelving, some only have two wheels on them, they are our best targets" said little Joey, "Tony, if you and Bert scamper up the legs of those shelves and push off the cheese, we will try to stop the wheels from rolling away".

"right young Bert, we're on!" said Tony, more than ready for the challenge.

Tony and Bert leapt up the first shelf that had only one cheese on it, stood at one side and using all their effort to push the wheel to the edge, that was the hard part done.

"Ready guys?" asked Tony.

"We're ready" replied big Joey.

"On the count of three and we push even harder than before but try not to hold the cheese with your paws, you wouldn't want to be dragged over the edge" said Tony, "One, Two, Threeeeeee".

Bert and Tony gave the cheese an almighty shove and it went toppling off the shelf, just missing big Joey by a couple of inches.

"Steady boys" said big Joey, "keep it on the edge and we can roll it to the pipe".

Donnie, little Joey and big Joey pushed the cheese wheel to the air conditioning pipe and lifted it a little to get it into the pipe, thankfully, it was small enough to fit, they hadn't thought of the 'What if it didn't fit?' idea.

Tony and Bert climbed back down from the shelf, making their way to the next cheese wheel, quickly running up the leg of the shelving.   This time, there were two wheels of cheese stacked one on top of the other.
"One at a time Bert" said Tony, "the others will be back soon".

They pushed the top cheese towards the edge of the bottom cheese, making use of the waxed paper between them.
"On three again?" asked Bert.
"Yes, worked perfectly last time" replied Tony. Again, they both pushed, giving it lots of effort but this cheese didn't need that due to the waxed paper.   It came flying off the shelf like a spaceship, spinning through the air, almost floating for a second or two before thundering towards the ground and the rest of them.
"Look out!" shouted little Joey, as he dived to push Donnie out of the way.

Luckily, the way the cheese came off the shelf meant that they didn't have far to roll it, it had pretty much rolled to the end pipe already.

"Two down" said Tony, pausing for an 'and' to his sentence, "Bert, how many more?".

"At least six" he replied, licking the cheese taste from his paws.

"six including those?" asked Tony.

"No, Tony, six more" said Bert.

"Oh Cheese!!" exclaimed Tony.

"Boys, can you tell us when you're going to push next time?" said big Joey, "Donnie nearly got cheesed!".

"Ooops!" said Tony, "are you ready now?"

"Yep, push it off when you're ready" said Donnie.

"One, Two…" said Tony.

"Oh just push the darn thing" said Bert, digging his back claws into the shelf for more grip.

Off went the cheese, this time with no danger to any of the others, in fact, it went as smoothly as the first one, you could say it was 'easy cheesy'.

"Another five more!" shouted Tony to big Joey.

"5?!" exclaimed big Joey.

"well, that's what Bert said and like little Joey said earlier, if it was only two, it's not really a heist and eight IS a nice round figure" replied

Tony, "round, get it?!".   Off he went, laughing to himself.

Donnie, big Joey and little Joey began rolling cheese wheel number three to the pipe, while Tony and Bert were taking a quick rest before moving on to the next shelf.

When they reached it, they put the cheese into position and pushed, albeit, a bit too hard, almost knocking the bag from the end of the pipe.
"WHOA!" said Dotty, who was trying to keep watch and hold the bag in place at the same time, "you nearly ripped the bag off the pipe then".
"One more then you need to change the bag" said little Joey, "that will make four cheeses in there".
"I don't think the bag will take more than three and it seems pointless renewing the bag just for one more cheese" said Dotty.
"well, just put a new bag on now and we'll get the other two in the last bag" said little Joey.
"Hang on, hang on" said Dotty, "my maths isn't what it used to be but that means there would be eight in total".

"That's what figure Bert came up with, he originally said two but I told him that it would hardly be a heist with so few" said little Joey.
"So, we have you to thank for that" said Dotty, "and how do you suggest we get it all back to the rabbit hole?".
"I'm working on that" replied little Joey.

They left the end of the pipe, leaving Dotty, literally spitting feathers, heading back to Tony and Bert, who were still resting, probably having a quick forty winks.

To their surprise, Tony and Bert were in place, ready to push off the next cheese wheel.
"You lot took your sweet time" said Bert.
"We had to tell Dotty what was happening or should I say, the amount of this stuff we are taking" said big Joey.
"Is it break time yet?" asked Donnie.
"Break time?!" replied big Joey, "this isn't a holiday camp!"
"You can eat when we all eat" added big Joey, "when we get back to the safety of the rabbit hole".

"Are we ready now?" asked Tony.

"Ready when you are" replied little Joey.

"One, Two…" said Tony, swiftly interrupted by Bert.

"Stop it with the counting already, it's like you're doing a sound check at a music festival, One Two, One Two" said Bert.

Tony began to push the cheese wheel, it wasn't really moving much until Bert started to push it too, which was only after realising, Tony's face was turning an unusual shade of purple.

"That was the hardest one yet" said Tony.

"It was" agreed Bert, knowing that it was his fault that Tony was doing all the work, "maybe counting isn't such a bad thing after all".

"Why the sudden change Bert?" asked Tony.

"Oh, no reason" replied Bert, smiling an innocent smile.

They pushed down another two cheese wheels from the same shelf and then had to climb down while waiting for the others to return from the pipe and moved around the corner, closer to the old air conditioning pipe.

"There's another two around the corner, they came down very easily" said Bert.

As soon as Bert had finished what he was saying, the distant bell, for the end of lunch break, sounded again.

"I have a feeling that the humans will be back soon" said Tony.

"Right boys, we all need to work together and get those cheeses in the bag" said big Joey.

"We've done our part" said Bert.

"I said ALL" said big Joey, "that's means YOU and Tony".

"But…" said Bert.

"No Buts!" said big Joey, "if we don't all help, someone will be caught by the humans for sure".

"Ok, ok, I get it" said Bert.

They all pushed the cheese wheels to the pipe, Donnie, big Joey and little Joey rolling one, Bert and Tony rolling the other, quickly getting them down the pipe into the bag.

"Change the bag Dotty" said Tony, "and we have to be much quieter now, I think the humans will be back soon"

"Roger!" replied Dotty, "I'll change the bag and await the last two cheeses".

"Roger?" asked Donnie, "Who's Roger?   Is it one of the humans that Dotty has seen outside and he's warning us?".

"Ha Ha Ha" said Tony, "it's a different way of saying Yes".

"Well, why didn't he just say that" said Donnie, "all this confusion makes my brain hurt".

"Tony, are you coming up?" asked Bert, already on the next shelf, waiting for Tony to help him push the cheese wheel from it.

"I'll be right there" replied Tony, thinking of what Donnie had said and still giggling.

It wasn't long before Tony had climbed up and standing next to Bert, who was already in position, to start the push.

"Ready boys?" asked Bert quietly.

"Yes" whispered little Joey in reply.

"One, Two, Three" said Bert.

Tony and Bert pushed the cheese wheel, which was easier than the first six, little did they realise that it was sitting waxed paper, well, not until they both slipped and went whizzing across the shelf, feet first into another cheese wheel.

"Wasn't expecting that!" said Tony, his left paw stuck in the outer part of the cheese coating.

"I wasn't either" said Bert.

"I'll just pop my paw out of this thing and we can get on with the job of getting it down" said Tony.

"We can't take that one now" said Bert, "it's broken".

"Broken? It's only a paw print" said Tony.

"Well I wouldn't eat it" said Bert, "it's not just a paw print, it's a RAT paw print, no offence".

"Wait a Fondueing minute" said Tony, "you say RAT like it's a bad thing".

"I didn't mean it to sound bad, I just wanted to say that most other cheese eaters wouldn't like any paw prints in their food" said Bert, almost choking on his words.

"One, Two…" said Bert, who was cut short by Tony.

"I'll do the counting!" said Tony.

After the count of three, Bert and Tony forced the last wheel over the shelf edge, on to the floor below.   Donnie, little Joey and big Joey rolled it away as they had done with the others and down the pipe as Tony and Bert began to climb down from the shelving units.

"We'll meet you at the pipe" said little Joey.

"Ok" said Bert, about to say something else, "HUMAN!" he squeaked before scrambling down the leg of the shelf.

Tony heard this and froze, he had figured out, if he could 'Play Dead', whatever the danger was, would soon go away.   Holding his breath, letting out the odd trump now and then, adding to the 'dead' effect, smelling like a rubbish bin that hasn't had its bag changed in a very long time.

The door creaked open further as a human could be seen standing just outside the doorway, about to walk into the cheese store.
"Yeah, I'm going to check the temperature of the store room and I'll be back out to start the new batch" said the human, now stood in the doorway, to one of the other humans.

He walked towards the area where Tony was laying still and holding his breath, by now gasping for air.
"The temperature is ok" said the Human, talking to himself, "oh dear, poor little fella, I'll have you in a much better place soon mate, just let me get a plastic bag to put you in" he added, looking at Tony's still, almost out of breath, body.

Off the man went, into the main part of the factory, to get a plastic bag.

Chapter 18
PIPES AWAY

Tony leapt to his feet, gasping for breath while slowly climbing down the leg of the shelves.

"Where is everyone?" Tony whispered.

"We're here Tony" said big Joey, stepping out of the shadows near the air conditioning pipe.

"Phew!   I thought you had gone already" said Tony.

"No Tony, we would never leave anyone behind" said little Joey, also stepping out from the shadows near the pipe.

"We have all we came for" said Bert, "let's get out of here before that human comes back", as he took a huge leap into the end of the air conditioning pipe, "Jeronimooooooo!".

He slid down with such speed that Dotty thought it was another cheese wheel rolling down the pipe.

"What on earth?!" shrieked Dotty.

"you didn't take the bag off the pipe Dotty" said Bert.

"Right you are" said Dotty, totally oblivious to what had just happened, "have we finished now?"
"Yes Dotty" said Bert, "now get me out of this bag of cheese".

Dotty removed the bag from the air conditioning pipe, to find Bert, standing on one of the Gorgonzola wheels.
Bert hopped out of the bag and shook himself, before licking the cheese smell from his fur, savouring every little cheese morsel that he found.
"Boys?" said Dotty, "you can come out now, Bert is safely through".
"Tony, you go now, Donnie you go next and then little Joey, I'll go last" said big Joey.

Tony slid himself down the pipe and came flying out the other end, bouncing into the full cheese bags that Dotty had stack outside.
"Jeronimohno!!" exclaimed Donnie, as he went down the pipe realising that he wasn't quite 'flying' down it, more, 'rippling' down it and getting stuck in the end of the pipe.

Little Joey was next to go, "see you on the outside Papa" he said, giving big Joey a little hug.

"Go quickly" said big Joey, "the human may be back anytime now", shoving little Joey down the pipe into a stuck Donnie, who was now talking to himself due to his very short attention span. POP!!

Donnie was no longer blocking the pipe but made a soft landing for little Joey, who landed on his, soft, round stomach, almost sinking into the downy fur.

Big Joey looked around to make sure that he hadn't been seen, just as he readied himself, the human came back through the door, carrying a plastic bag to remove Tony from the shelf and looking somewhat puzzled that he had disappeared.

While he was distracted, searching for Tony's 'Dead Body', big Joey slowly lowered himself into the air conditioning pipe, then let go of the edge to slide, "weeeeeee!" he said to himself as quietly as he could.

"Are we all here now?" asked Dotty.

"Yes" replied big Joey, "this is Tony, I know him from a long time ago, way back in the Verminage, long story Dotty but I'll tell you all

119

about it later".

"I've seen him hanging around the scarecrow in the field on the odd occasion" said Dotty, "I thought he was some sort of criminal, he looked around a lot".

"That's my SRS training" said Tony.

"SRS?!" asked Dotty.

"Force of habit, Special Rat Service" replied Tony, "most other animals in these parts knew me many years ago, I've been in hiding for some time, I'm Tony 'The Rat' Gambino".

"THE Tony The Rat?" asked Dotty.

"Yes, do you know me Dotty?" Tony asked.

"There isn't an animal, in these here parts, that hasn't heard of Tony 'The Rat', animals of a certain age" said Dotty, "your reputation is well known".

"Oh, please stop" said Tony, "I can feel my cheeks going a scarlet shade of red".

"Well, all has gone well so far" said Donnie, "but how are we going to get all this cheese back to the rabbit hole?".

"Good question Donnie" said Dotty, "Bert, how exactly are we going to get this cheese back out of here?".

"Ahem" said Bert clearing his voice, "Dotty is going to carry the sacks one at a time, back to the rabbit hole, they'll be too heavy to carry together".

"HOO HOO!" exclaimed Dotty, "I didn't think we were stealing so much cheese as this".

"Well, it was little Joey's idea, I mean, there's no point stealing one or two now is there?" said Bert, looking at little Joey for a little support.

"We changed the plans slightly" said little Joey.

"Well you could have told me!" said Dotty.

"It was a lastminute thing" said little Joey.

"Never mind all this bickering" said big Joey, "let's get this stuff shifted and get back for some food".

"Here, here!" said Donnie, in total agreement, his stomach making more noise than any stomach should EVER make.

Bert went to tie the sacks securely for the flight back to the rabbit hole, sneaking a lick of a cheese wheel.

"I'll take one back now and then come back" said Dotty, "will you all be waiting here when I get back?"

"Yes" shouted Bert, tying up the last sack "we have to make sure those humans from the factory come and take their cheese back".

Dotty went towards the first sack, took it in his claws and flapped his long powerful wings, hovering and struggling to get the sack off the ground.

"HOOOOOOO!" said Dotty under the strain, finally taking flight properly.

"That looked like effort" said big Joey.

"He'll be okay" said Bert, "what we will do to pass the time is my worry".

"I Spy with my…." started Donnie.

"Stop!" shouted Bert, "can we find something ELSE to do?".

"Well, what do you suggest?" said Donnie, "I was just trying to keep us busy and out of trouble".

"What about a game of snap?" said Tony.

"Snap?!" said big Joey, "no one has got any cards".

With that, Tony pulled out the smallest set of cards you could ever imagine, from under the fur of his armpit.

"So, who's playing?" asked Tony.

"Deal us all in" said little Joey, "we can't do much else while waiting for Dotty".

"I had made a suggestion of…." Said Donnie.

"WE KNOW!" said little Joey and Bert almost at the same time.

"Snap, it is then!" said Donnie, still upset that he couldn't play 'I Spy'.

Tony dealt the cards and turned over the card to start the game, they played for a while, in the outside lights of the factory, most of the time in silence, except the flick of the cards as they turned them over and the occasional 'Snap!' thrown in, sometimes not even on the right cards.
"HOO HOO HOO!" sounded Dotty from above.
"Sounds like Dotty's back" said Tony, playing his last card of the game.

Dotty landed with the grace of an elephant, clattering the end of the air conditioning duct.
"I know you wanted more little Joey, but I don't think I can manage more than two more bags" said Dotty, breathlessly, "but I do think I will two take this time, wasn't too bad once I had lifted off" he added.
"We were hoping to take back three full bags Dotty but, but eight cheese wheels will be enough for us to trade and keep some for Bert" Little Joey said.

Whilst Dotty prepared himself for the huge task ahead, the others discussed what they would do, I mean, it wasn't fair that they would ask Dotty to carry then all back home to the rabbit hole. "Right Dotty, when you have set off, we will find a safe way back" said Big Joey. "HOO RIGHTY!" exclaimed Dotty.

As Dotty took to the sky for the last time, with the effort of a tiny Ant lifting a huge leaf, Bert, Donnie, little Joey, big Joey and Tony, prepared to make their way across the carpark, before the sun came over the distant horizon.

Chapter 19

QUICK, TO THE RAT CAVE!

Tony the Rat led the way in the fading light of the factory carpark, into the gloom of the night, towards the direction of his hideout.

"This isn't the way back to the Rabbit hole" said Bert, "where are we going Tony?"

"No Bert, you're right, we need to lay low until it's safe" replied Tony, "the humans may try to look for the missing cheese, the smell on our clothes would leave a dog friendly trail, back to the Rabbit hole and we may all be eaten!"

"Please don't mention food" said Donnie, his stomach making more noise that a heard of wild buffalo, "I could chew off my own leg, I'm THAT hungry".

"Ok Tony, where are we actually going?" asked Big Joey.

"I have a secret hideaway that I like to call 'The Rat Cave'" said Tony, with a little smile crossing his face.

"Well, we had better get there before it gets light or before the humans come looking for us" Bert said.

Tony stepped up the pace to ensure they were at the hideaway long before the sun had risen and before the humans had even noticed that any cheese was missing.
Within, what appeared to be a matter of minutes, they had arrived at the Rat Cave.
"We're here!" declared Tony, looking at the confused faces of the tired rabble following him.
"Where's the entrance?" asked Donnie, his feet throbbing like a thumb that had taken the hammers' beating that was meant for the nail.
"I need to put my rear feet up, or someone else is going to get my lucky feet", he added, thinking that his feet would drop off any moment now.

"Here's the entrance" said Tony, pulling on what looked like an old piece of string.
The grass around the opening shook as the stone door swing open, thankfully, it was big enough for Donnie to squeeze through.
"Come on in" said Tony, "make yourselves at home" as he walked into the passage that lead into the large dome shaped room.

"If we're laying low here, where are we going to sleep?" asked Bert.

"Well, Bert" said Tony, "there are no other rooms, so we will all have to sleep in this one, oh, and there's only one main way in and out for security but there is a secret tunnel, should we need it".

"Where is the tunnel Tony?" asked Donnie, a little panicked at the prospect of being trapped underground, even though he lives in a Rabbit hole, also underground!

"It's a Seeeeecret!" replied Tony, "otherwise, it wouldn't be".

Donnie at this point, was totally confused at what was going on, let alone what he has just been told and went off in the search of food.

Bert pulled out a small lump of cheese that he had taken from the factory and stuffed in the fur beneath his chin, a sort of beard cupboard.

"mmmmm!" Bert delighted, "this is absolutely gooooor…."

"Bert? What are you eating" asked Big Joey

"erm, well, erm" Bert answered, a little embarrassed and red faced.

"He's eating cheese" said Little Joey, "he broke some from a wheel that we decided not to take"

"When were you going to tell us that you had food?" asked Donnie, who, by this time had returned from his effortless food hunt, his stomach almost asking the same question, but in a mumbling sound.
"Oh Dear" said Bert, "I am going to share, I totally forgot"

Bert broke a piece off for all of them and kept the smallest piece for himself, after all, he had already eaten some cheese.
"I don't even like cheese" said Little Joey
"Me neither" added Big Joey and Donnie together.

Tony, on the other hand, was like Bert, so wrapped up in the moment of cheese fumes and creamy bitterness of the matured Gorgonzola. After eating the tiny morsels that they had, they all collapsed in the large room, swollen bellies pointing toward the ceiling.   Soon they were all sleeping, with the odd snore and snuffle.

The next two days passed quite quickly, although they didn't do much whilst hiding away, they were all sleepy and ready to go home, probably to sleep some more, well, at least in a bed.

"I'm going out to see if there are any humans or other problems that will stop us leaving" said Big Joey, as he walked down the passage that they had arrived through.

Everyone else didn't pay that much attention, they were all too busy, stretching, yawning and trying to wake up properly.

A few moments passed, Big Joey returned from the far end of the passage, his smile running from ear to ear.

"What's with the big smile?" asked Little Joey.

"No reason" said Big Joey, still carrying his huge smile.

"Papa!" said Donnie, "Why the big silly grin?".

"I was just thinking what we have done in the past week and the next part of our adventure home" said Big Joey.

"Will we set off now?" asked Tony, "is it safe Big Joey?".

"Yep!" said Big Joey, "we're good to go".

Bert lead the way, back down the passage to the huge door of the entrance.

"How do we open this thing?" Bert asked.

"See the root on the left-hand side?" replied Tony, "give it a good old pull and the door will open".

Bert grabbed hold of the root with both his paws
and pulled with all his might, but, nothing,
nothing budged, nothing at all.   He looked at
Tony puzzled as to why it wouldn't open.
"Not that one Bert" said Tony, "it's the other
one, next to the one you are trying to pull out of
the soil!".

Chapter 20

TIME TO HEAD HOME

Bert took a hold of the other root and with little effort, the door swing open to reveal the brightness of the late afternoon sun.

"I thought we were travelling at night" said Little Joey, "undercover of darkness?".
"No, Big Joey and I thought it would be best to travel during the day so we don't get lost, the Rat Cave is literally, in the middle of nowhere" said Tony.
"Now I get it" said Little Joey, "let's do it".
Big Joey took the lead to take the gang back home, slowly edging out of the cave watching for any possible hazards, closely followed by Bert, Tony, Donnie and Little Joey keeping an eye out from the back.

As the door of the Rat Cave swung closed behind them, which made Donnie jump with fright, the gang made their way back through the surrounding fields back to the Rabbit hole and Mrs Albino, trying to avoid perils along the way, as this was a different route to the one they took to get to the cheese factory.

Through the fields of wheat, into the pumpkin field, which was a struggle, avoiding the roots and vines of the plants.

"Are we there yet?" moaned Bert, getting tired from the jumping over this and that.

"Shhhhh!" said Tony, "there are other dangers out there".

"What dangers?" asked Donnie, again, shaking in his fur and almost wishing he hadn't asked.

"Well" said Tony, "there are stray cats".

"What?!" said Donnie, "what do you mean, Stray Cats, what have they strayed from?" he added naively.

"hahahaha" chuckled Bert, "they haven't strayed from anything, it means that they don't have a home like we do, they're WILD!!"

Donnie's eyes grew so big with fright that they almost resembled the moon in size, as they flicked from side to side, looking for these scary creatures.

Into the Maize field they went, only a couple more fields and hedgerows to conquer.

The Maize grew so high that underneath was almost as black as coal, they could barely see eachother.   "Ow!!" screeched Bert.

"What's the matter with you?" asked Little Joey.
"Tony stood on my foot, its already sore from all the walking" added Bert.
"I'm sorry dear boy, I thought I'd trodden on a twig or something, didn't realise it was your foot" said Tony, apologetically.

Bert decided to hang back and walk alongside Little Joey, who was walking at the rear.
"Almost there" said Big Joey with a happy tone to his voice, which was unusual for him.
"Thankfully" replied Little Joey from the back, "Thanks to Tony, I'm almost having to carry Bert with his sore foot" he added, Bert leaning heavily on his waist.
Through the bracken hedge they crawled, getting the odd scrape and scuff from the thorns of the branches.
"HOOOOOOO!" they heard from above.
"Dotty's here" cried Donnie, somewhat elated.
But it wasn't Dotty, it was a different Owl, one that none of them recognised.
In that instance, the Owl noticed them moving out of the bracken, into the light of the moon.
WHOOOOOOOSH!!

The Owl swooped down, narrowly missing Bert by millimetres, his fur rippling in the breeze of the owl's wings.

"That was close" said Little Joey.

"What was?" asked Bert, totally oblivious of what had just happened.

"You didn't see that?" asked Little Joey.

"See what?" asked Bert, still no idea of how close the danger was.

"Doesn't matter" said Little Joey, dragging Bert along as he sped up to the rest of them.

WHOOOOOOOOSH!!

The Owl swooped again, this time, just missing the top of Big Joey's right ear.   It was nowhere near his left ear, as this was flopping down at the side of his head from an old bare paw boxing accident years ago.

They all quickened the pace as they entered the final field, the carrot field, scurrying in a zig-zag pattern, in an attempt to avoid being eaten by the unknown Owl assailant.

MIOW! MIOW! MIOW!

Three loud screeches heard in the distance.

"What in Holy Rabbits dungarees was that?" asked Bert, still unaware of the dangerous Owl, flying overhead.

"I'm guessing it's the stray cats" said Tony, "the ones I have told you about"

Donnie's eyes, if this was possible, grew even bigger than before.
"We need to be home now" said Donnie, shaking like a glass of strawberry milk, "this isn't an adventure now, it's more of a ghost train!", a phrase he had once overheard when the Circus came to the village.
They were in sight of the Rabbit hole, the light from within, shining upwards, into the darkness of the night, like a homing beacon for them to follow.

With one last spurt of energy, they all bounded into the Rabbit hole, tumbling down as the Owl took one final swoop.
"Fiorela!", shouted Big Joey, "We are home safe and have we got a story to tell you!!"
"I have carrot casserole on the stove and a little cheese snack for the cheese eaters" replied Mama, "I am so glad that you are all home safe, Dotty dropped off the cheese sacks just outside, he stayed long enough to tell me so, but I haven't seen him for a couple of days, not since that other, larger Owl has been flying around"

TO BE CONTINUED……

Printed in Great Britain
by Amazon

32498729R00079